Engaging Tales for Bright Boys

Empowering Stories on Confidence, Camaraderie, and Bravery for Young Minds

Casper Willow

Contact Information: amazingbooksforkids.fun@gmail.com

ISBN: 979-8-89292-221-0

Contents

Introduction

Welcome to a world where imagination knows no bounds, and adventure awaits at every turn.

This book is your passport to a journey unlike any other, where heroes rise, mysteries unfold, and the power of friendship is the greatest magic of all.

Designed for the young and young at heart, our stories are woven with lessons of courage, kindness, and the endless possibilities of belief in oneself. Dive into these pages, and let's embark on an unforgettable adventure together!

The Extraordinary Object

Chapter 1: The Stormy Beginning

Boom!

The first thunderclap rocked the school, sending shivers down the walls and making the windows dance. During this wild orchestra, Leon's heart was pounding like a drum in his chest. His eyes, wide with a mix of awe and anxiety, were locked onto the storm's fury outside. But his real fear lay hidden at the bottom of his backpack: an old compass, worn with the patina of countless adventures, its surface a map of tiny scratches, each a silent witness to tales untold. This compass, a gift from his seafaring father, was a precious link to the thrilling stories of battling ocean storms. It symbolized the unbreakable bond between them, yet it remained tucked away, unseen, as Leon grappled with the newness of everything around him – the new house and the unknown streets, the different faces on the school bus, and the sea of strangers that were his classmates. His shyness was a heavy cloak, making even the thought of sharing his compass feel like lifting mountains.

But today, Leon faced an even bigger challenge than the roaring storm: the "EXTRAORDINARY OBJECT" competition. Just a few days earlier, his teacher had unveiled this special event, where students were to showcase objects dear to their hearts. The winner would be awarded a magnificent golden trophy, gleaming like a beacon of achievement. The idea of speaking about his compass in front of classmates he'd only known for a few weeks made Leon's heart sink. What if they laughed at his old, battered compass? What if they teased him?

Chapter 2: Show and Tell

As the storm outside howled and whistled, painting the sky with shades of anger, the classroom was a cauldron of excitement and chatter. Hanna beamed as she showed a photo of her dog Hugo, her tail-wagging, joy-bringing best friend. Alex, with dreams as high as the sky, flaunted his baseball jersey signed by a legend, his eyes sparkling with ambition.

Then came Richard's turn. With a swagger that commanded attention, he stepped forward, revealing a watch that shimmered like a star. "Check this out, it's super expensive!" he declared with a grin.

The teacher, with a knowing smile, gently nudged, "And why is it extraordinary to you, Richard?" With the confidence of a king, Richard boasted, "Because my dad says it's a watch for the rich. That's what makes it special."

The teacher, eyes warm with wisdom, responded softly, "It's certainly a beautiful watch. But remember, this contest celebrates objects that hold personal significance. Think of something that made you grow, feel proud, or cherish a memory. True value lies there."

The classroom fell silent as Richard pondered, his face clouding with thought. The others looked on, their young minds wrestling with the idea of wealth versus worth.

Stepping closer, the teacher added, "Imagine having everything money could buy, but no one to share your laughter and dreams with. Happiness isn't just about possessions, Richard. It's about the moments we share and the love we spread. That's what makes us truly rich."

A flicker of understanding passed through Richard's eyes, in that fleeting moment, Richard realized that he would gladly trade the watch's material value for the precious moments he could share with his father if he worked less and was more present in his life.

The show-and-tell resumed.

Jamal proudly held up his brother's old baseball cap, a token of admiration and sibling love. Kyiara shared a box of coins from across the globe, each a gateway to fantastical worlds and dreams, gifts from her globe-trotting aunt.

As the contest unfolded in the bustling classroom, the storm outside gathered its own menacing momentum. The sky, painted in strokes of angry gray, loomed over the school as distant thunderclaps echoed like ominous drums. Yet, within the classroom's walls, the students' excitement drowned out the brewing tempest. Each presentation unveiled a new layer of personal stories and cherished memories.

As the spotlight of attention inched closer to him, Leon's heart raced against time. The old compass, a silent testament to his father's seafaring adventures and their bond, lay hidden in his backpack, its presence both comforting and daunting.

The classroom was a kaleidoscope of stories and dreams, each student's object a window into their world.

Serena, with a grace beyond her years, brought forward a beautifully craft-ed drum, its surface adorned with intricate designs. She tapped it gently, and the room filled with the resonant sounds of her heritage. Each beat was a heartbeat of history, echoing the tales of her ancestors. Her eyes sparkled with pride as she shared how her grandparents had taught her to play, connecting her to a lineage of music and tradition.

Max, whose resilience shone through every challenge, held up a pair of worn crutches. Each one bore the marks of his journey - from reliance to independence. He shared his story with quiet strength, telling of the days before he received his prosthetic leg, how these crutches had been his con-stant companions. They were not just tools for mobility; they were sym-bols of his journey towards self-reliance. Max's story, brief yet profound, was a testament to enduring courage and the triumph of determination over adversity.

Olivia unfolded a vibrant, hand-woven blanket, each thread a story, each color a memory. She explained how her family had woven it together, a patchwork of cultural richness and familial love. The blanket was more than fabric; it was a tapestry of her life, each stitch a connection to her roots and the hands that nurtured her.

Lucas, with a twinkle of mischief in his eyes, proudly showcased his sleek biker glasses. He shared dreams of future road trips with his older brother, and this pair of glass were reflecting the promise of adventure and the bond of brotherhood. The glasses symbolized a world waiting to be discovered.

Sophia's case of glowing mushrooms and rare plants was a miniature ecosystem, each leaf and spore a silent witness to the wonders of nature. She spoke of her love for the environment, her voice a melody of passion and care. The plants were not just specimens; they were her companions.

Tommy, always the class clown, presented a rusty old wrench with a flourish. He joked about his 'incredible' mechanical skills, but his eyes softened as he spoke of his father. The wrench was a symbol of their bond, of weekends spent tinkering in the garage, learning the art of fixing and building. It was a token of love and shared experiences.

As each student shared their piece of the world, Leon's feelings of isolation and apprehension deepened. His compass, steeped in personal history but outwardly unremarkable, seemed dwarfed by his classmates' extraordinary items. The weight of doubt and the fear of being misunderstood or ridiculed loomed over him.

As the spotlight of attention inched closer to him, Leon's heart raced against time. Mrs. Mitchell, perceptive and supportive, offered him an encouraging nod, her eyes conveying a message of unwavering belief in his worth. Drawing a shaky breath, Leon reached into his backpack. His fingers traced the familiar contours of the compass, each scratch and dent a story of resilience and guidance.

Chapter 3: The Tornado Strikes

Just as he was about to present the compass, the piercing wail of the tornado siren cut through the room, silencing his nascent bravery.

The classroom, once buzzing with excitement, plunged into a frenzy as the tornado siren's shrill cry pierced the air. Mrs. Mitchell's voice, firm yet laced with concern, cut through the chaos. "Under the desks, now!" she commanded.

The children's laughter and chatter were replaced by the sound of shuffling feet and heavy breaths. Leon's heart raced as he clutched his backpack, the compass inside now an afterthought in the face of imminent danger. He dove under his desk, his eyes wide with fear, as the world outside seemed to turn hostile.

The wind outside roared like an angry beast, battering against the windows with relentless fury. The classroom, a safe haven just moments ago, now felt like a fragile shell amidst the storm's wrath.

Leon's moment, the opportunity to share his story and the significance of the compass, was swept away in the tide of panic. In the dim light, he could see the outlines of his classmates, huddled and tense, their faces etched with anxiety.

Mrs. Mitchell, receiving an urgent call from the principal, left the classroom with a promise to return as soon as possible. In her absence, the focus on the contest waned, overshadowed by the ominous howls and gusts of the tempest outside. Leon clutched the compass, its presence a silent reminder of the unforeseen challenges they were about to face.

Chapter 4: A Test of Courage

The full fury of the tornado struck with a force that was both terrifying and awe-inspiring. A tree, uprooted and wild, crashed against the classroom window, its branches clawing at the barrier between safety and chaos. The electric lights flickered and succumbed to the storm's wrath, plunging the room into an eerie darkness, illuminated sporadically by the furious dance of lightning.

As smoke began to snake its way under the classroom door, a collective realization dawned - they were trapped, with a raging fire on one side and a blocked window on the other. Fear and confusion mingled in the air, as thick as the smoke that threatened to engulf them.

The situation inside the classroom escalated rapidly. Flames, like greedy fingers, reached for the edges of the window, while the smoke grew denser, stinging their eyes and clawing at their throats. The air, thick and acrid, became increasingly difficult to breathe.

In this moment of crisis, Leon felt an unexpected weight in his hand - the compass.

Amid chaos and fear, Leon's voice, which usually quivered with uncertainty, rose with unexpected strength. He pulled out the compass, its needle dancing wildly and said, "This compass can guide us," his voice firm with resolve, echoing his father's tales of navigating treacherous seas.

"But it's too dark to see!" cried Richard, his voice trembling.

Sophia, her eyes wide with realization, held up her jar of bioluminescent mushrooms. "These are Foxfire Fungi," she exclaimed. "They glow in the dark!" The eerie, soft light from the mushrooms cast a ghostly glow, allowing Leon to read the compass outside the classroom.

They reached the door, only to find the doorknob scalding hot. "We can't touch that!" gasped Jamal.

ENGAGING TALES FOR BRIGHT BOYS

Tommy, gripping his trusty wrench, stepped forward. "I've got this," he declared, wrapping the wrench around the doorknob, and turning it with a grunt. The door swung open, revealing an aisle shrouded in thick smoke.

"We can't go through that; we won't be able to breathe!" Lucas coughed, his eyes stinging from the smoke.

Olivia, quick-thinking, unfurled her vibrant blanket. "Use this to cover your mouths," she suggested. They all grabbed a piece of the fabric, pressing it to their faces as they crawled low, seeking cleaner air.

Through the smoky haze, Leon struggled to see the way forward. Lucas, removing his biker glasses, handed them to Leon. "These might help you see better," he said, a note of hope in his voice.

Leon put on the glasses, and the world became clearer. Guided by the dim light of Sophia's mushrooms and the direction of the compass, they moved cautiously forward.

"Which way now, Leon?" asked Kyiara, her voice barely above a whisper.

Leon glanced at the compass, then pointed. "This way, towards the east wing. It should be safer."

Chapter 5: Unity and Escape

As they navigated the smoke-filled corridors, each obstacle they encountered was met with a solution born from their shared objects and experiences. The steady rhythm of Serena's drum had served as a beacon guiding their footsteps through the smoke-filled, disorienting corridors.

Max, leaning on his crutches, used one to push debris out of their path.

Guided by Leon's steady hand and the faint glow of the mushrooms, the group navigated through the maze of smoke-filled corridors. Each obstacle they encountered was met with a solution born of their collective strengths and the unique properties of their extraordinary objects.

As they reached the ground floor, the first glimmer of hope emerged - they were close to escaping the fiery trap that had ensnared them.

Their path to safety, however, was thwarted by a collapsed wall, its debris a formidable barrier to their escape.

In a moment of desperation, they spotted a potential way out - a window, albeit perilously high.

A plan was quickly formed, utilizing Olivia's blanket as a makeshift rope. One by one, they carefully lowered themselves down to safety. Max, his confidence momentarily faltering due to his prosthetic leg, was the last to make the leap. Below, his classmates stood ready, the blanket stretched taut as a safety net. With a mixture of fear and trust, Max jumped, landing safely into the cradle of the blanket, held firm by the hands of his friends.

They were out and all safe!

Chapter 6: Leon's Triumph

Outside, the fresh air was a balm to their smoke-filled lungs.

The sight of firefighters and the relief of safety enveloped them in a wave of gratitude and disbelief. They had made it out, together, their bond strengthened by the trial they had just endured.

A few minutes later, Mrs. Mitchell ran towards them, her eyes brimming with tears of relief and pride. She gathered them in a group hug, expressing her gratitude for their safety and bravery.

Leon, once the shy new kid, was now seen in a new light. His classmates looked at him with respect and admiration.

A few weeks after the harrowing experience, the students of Mrs. Mitchell's class were back in their classroom. The class buzzed with a mixture of excitement and reflection as they came together to commemorate their collective bravery during the tornado.

Mrs. Mitchell stood at the front of the assembly, her eyes scanning over her students with a mix of pride and affection. She cleared her throat, and the room fell silent. "Today, we are here to acknowledge an extraordinary act of courage and leadership," she began, her voice steady but filled with emotion.

"Leon, with his quick thinking and the guidance of his compass, played a pivotal role in leading all kids to safety. You and your compass saved everyone and for this reason, you were unanimously declared the winner of the 'EXTRAORDINARY OBJECT' contest."

As Leon's classmates cheered for him, the room erupted in applause. Leon, who wasn't accustomed to this kind of attention, blushed profusely. He looked around at his new friends, their faces beaming with pride and gratitude. With a heart full of emotions, he stepped forward.

"Mrs. Mitchell, thank you," Leon began, his voice clear and confident. "But I couldn't have done anything without everyone here. We all played a part in this. Serena's drum, Max's crutches, Olivia's blanket, Lucas's glasses, Sophia's mushrooms, Tommy's wrench, and the courage of the others... Each of these elements helped us escape the tornado. We survived because we worked together. "He paused, his gaze falling upon the gleaming golden trophy perched on the table. "I believe this trophy belongs to all of us. Let's keep it in our classroom as a reminder of what we can accomplish together. This victory is not just mine; it belongs to all of us."

The room was silent for a moment, and then the applause resumed, louder and more heartfelt than before.

The trophy was placed in a special spot in the classroom, shining not just as a symbol of victory, but as a testament to the strength they found in unity and the courage they discovered within themselves.

The Secret of the Story

We can achieve wonderful things when we work together.

What extraordinary object would you have brought to the contest?

The Guardian of the Library

Chapter 1: A World Turned Upside Down

In Maplewood, a town as friendly as a summer day, lived a 10-year-old boy named James. His world, once filled with childhood wonders, had changed dramatically four years ago. James, with his mop of unruly brown hair and eyes that could light up with mischief or cloud over with sadness, missed his father deeply.

James's father had been more than just a parent; he was the mastermind behind their grandest adventures and the creator of their most cherished moments. Together, they had turned the backyard into wild jungles and distant planets. His father would crouch behind bushes, pretending to be a prowling tiger or an alien explorer, making James squeal with excitement and a touch of delightful fear.

Their weekends were filled with activities, each one a chapter in the grand book of memories James now clung to. They would spend hours in the garage, surrounded by tools and laughter, as they built model airplanes. Each model was a testament to their teamwork, with James's father teaching him how to meticulously paint the tiny figures and glue the delicate parts together. They would hold competitions, seeing whose plane could glide the furthest across the yard, both running after the soaring models with unbridled joy.

On clear nights, James's father would set up the old telescope they had bought together from a garage sale. They would take turns peering through it, marveling at the moon's craters and making up names for the stars. His father's stories about constellations and astronauts fueled James's fascination with space. These were the moments when the universe seemed to unfold just for them, a father and son sharing in the awe of the vast, starry sky.

Inside the house, James's room was a museum of these shared experiences. Model airplanes hung from the ceiling, each one a trophy of their shared passion. The telescope still stood by the window, though it hadn't been used since his father's passing. And there, in the corner, was the bookshelf filled with encyclopedias about space and aviation, gifts from his father that James treasured.

Life had taken a sharp turn when James's father fell ill. It was a swift and heartbreaking change, leaving James and his mother, Sarah, in a world that suddenly felt less colorful, less vibrant. Sarah, with her kind eyes and gentle voice, had tried to fill the void as best as she could. A year ago, she had remarried, hoping to bring some normalcy back into their lives. Mike, her new husband, was a good man in his late 30s, patient and well-meaning.

He tried to connect with James, offering to participate in activities and attempting to create new memories.

But for James, these gestures, though well-intentioned, felt like an intrusion. He was polite yet distant, often retreating to his room, where he could be with his thoughts and memories. James couldn't see Mike as anything other than a reminder of what he had lost. The model planes and the telescope were symbols of a past that he wasn't ready to move on from, relics of a time when laughter was abundant, and his father was by his side.

As the days grew shorter and the anniversary of his father's passing neared, James felt the weight of his grief more acutely. He longed for the days of his father's warm smiles and the adventures they shared. Unbeknownst to James, life was about to take another turn, one that would challenge his perceptions and lead him on a journey of healing and acceptance.

Chapter 2: The Tipping Point

James sat at the dinner table, fidgeting with his spoon. The room was filled with the clatter of dishes and the low hum of everyday conversation. Sarah, his mom, was talking about her day at work, but James was hardly listening. His mind was on the new video game he had been forbidden to play during weekdays, a rule Mike, his stepdad, had firmly enforced.

"James, did you finish your homework?" Mike asked, passing the salad bowl.

"Yeah, it's done," James replied, not meeting his gaze.

"Great. Maybe after dinner, you can help me with the dishes instead of rushing to your room," Mike suggested with a smile, trying to make light of the chore.

James rolled his eyes. "But I have a level to beat on my game. I've been waiting all day."

Mike's tone became firmer. "We agreed, no video games on school nights. You need to stick to the rules."

The mundane conversation quickly escalated. James felt a surge of frustration. "It's just a game! Why can't I play for just half an hour?"

"Because rules are rules, James. We need to be consistent," Mike insisted.

"You're not fair! You're always telling me what to do!" James's voice rose, his irritation growing.

Sarah interjected, trying to calm the situation. "James, we just want what's best for you."

"But you never listen to what I want!" James retorted; his voice tinged with defiance.

Mike sighed. "I'm trying to be a good parent here, James."

That was the last straw. James stood up abruptly, knocking his chair back. "You're not my dad! You can't tell me what to do!" he yelled; the words charged with all the pent-up emotions he had been holding back.

The room fell silent. Sarah's face was a mix of shock and sadness. Mike looked hurt but composed himself quickly. "James, I know I'm not your dad, but..."

James didn't wait for him to finish. He stormed out of the kitchen, his heart pounding with a mix of anger and grief. He grabbed his jacket and dashed out of the house, slamming the door behind him.

Chapter 3: A Cold Night

As he ran into the cool night, James's thoughts were a chaotic blend of anger, sadness, and a deep longing for the days when his dad was still around. The familiar streets of Maplewood blurred past him as he ran, not knowing where he was going, just needing to get away.

This impulsive exit marked the beginning of a new chapter in James's life, one filled with unexpected turns and revelations that would challenge him in ways he never imagined.

James's breath came out in clouds as he ran, his heart racing with a cocktail of fear and defiance. The frosty night air bit at his skin, and a regretful thought about his forgotten jacket flickered in his mind. The streets of Maplewood, usually so familiar and comforting, now seemed alien and indifferent to his turmoil.

As he wandered aimlessly, trying to outrun his emotions, James noticed a warm, inviting glow emanating from the Maplewood Library. He paused; his gaze drawn to the beacon of light in the chilly darkness. The library, with its towering shelves and silent halls, had once been a frequent escape, a place to lose himself in stories when the real world became too much.

With a heavy sigh, mixed with a longing for solace, James pushed open the library's doors. A wave of warmth and the familiar scent of books immediately enveloped him, offering a temporary refuge from the cold and his own troubled thoughts. He wandered through the aisles, his eyes skimming over the spines of countless books, each a portal to another world.

James wasn't really there to read, but he didn't want to draw attention to himself. He randomly picked a book off a shelf, its title barely registering in his mind. He found a secluded desk in a quiet corner and sat down, opening the book without really seeing the words. His mind was elsewhere, replaying the night's argument, each word echoing with pain and confusion.

James's eyes fluttered open to a world bathed in shadows and silvery moonlight. The library, so familiar and welcoming by day, had transformed into an enchanting maze of books and secrets in the night. He sat up, disoriented, realizing that the library had closed while he was lost in thought. The only light came from the moon, casting long, ghostly shadows through the high windows.

Chapter 4: Meeting the Guardian

Rubbing his eyes, James stood up, his legs stiff from sitting too long. As he looked around, the realization dawned on him that hours must have passed while he was lost in sleep. The library, now shrouded in darkness, felt vast and mysterious, a stark contrast to the familiar haven he knew. He wound his way through the aisles, his footsteps echoing softly in the quiet.

As he rounded a corner, his heart skipped a beat. There, in the dim light, stood an old man. He had kind eyes that twinkled with a hint of mischief and a gentle smile that immediately put James at ease. The man's presence was both surprising and oddly comforting.

"I'm the guardian of this library," the man said in a soft, soothing voice. His words carried a weight of wisdom and a touch of intrigue.

James blinked in surprise. "The guardian?" he echoed, curiosity piquing his interest despite his initial intention to leave quickly.

"Yes," the old man replied, a playful note in his voice. "Every library has one, though we often go unnoticed. But you, young man, have stayed past our closing hours. Might I see your library card? Just a formality, to ensure you're not here with ill intent."

James fumbled in his pocket and produced his library card, handing it over. The guardian inspected it with a nod.

"James," he said, reading the name on the card. "You seem troubled. It's rare for someone to find themselves locked in here after hours. Is everything alright?"

James hesitated for a moment, unsure how much to reveal to this stranger. But there was something about the guardian's kind eyes and warm smile that made him feel like he could trust him. Taking a deep breath, James began to explain.

Chapter 5: Sharing Secrets

"It's my stepdad," James started, his voice a mix of frustration and sadness. "We had an argument at dinner. It was stupid, really. He set these new rules about no video games on school nights, and I... I just lost it."

The guardian nodded, encouraging him to continue.

"I yelled at him," James admitted, his voice dropping. "I told him he's not my dad and that he can't tell me what to do. I didn't mean to say it, but I was just so angry."

There was a long pause as James gathered his thoughts. "Ever since my dad passed away, everything's changed. My mom remarried, and Mike... he's a good guy, but he's not my dad. I miss the way things used to be."

The guardian listened intently, his expression one of understanding. "Loss can leave a deep void in our hearts," he said softly. "It's natural to feel anger and sadness. But remember, James, those we love never truly leave us. They live on in our memories and the love they've given us."

James nodded, feeling a sense of relief as he shared his feelings.

The guardian, sensing James's need for guidance, leaned in slightly. "James, let me share a story with you. It's about a young tree that grew in the shadow of an old oak. The young tree often felt overshadowed and unnoticed. But the old oak would say, 'Use my shade to grow strong until you can reach the sunlight on your own.'"

James listened, the story piquing his interest.

"Your stepdad, like the young tree, is growing in a space that was once occupied by someone very significant - your father. He's not trying to overshadow but to find his own place in the sun, just as you are."

The guardian's words stirred something in James. He remembered his dad teaching him how to ride a bike. "When you're learning to ride, son, there will be wobbles and falls. But each time you get back up, you're one step closer to riding on your own," his dad had said.

"You see, James," the guardian continued, "life is a bit like learning to ride a bike. Your stepdad, he's also learning how to be part of your family, with its own wobbles and falls. It's a journey you're all on together."

James's thoughts turned to the many times his dad had encouraged him to be understanding and patient. He realized that these lessons applied not just to him, but to Mike as well.

"You might be right," James admitted, a thoughtful expression crossing his face. "I've been so focused on my own loss that I didn't see how hard it is for him too. My dad always said to look for the best in people."

The guardian's smile was gentle in the moonlight. "Remember, understanding and patience are keys that unlock many doors."

As James stood up, ready to leave, he felt a newfound appreciation for his father's wisdom and a better understanding of Mike's efforts. "Thanks for listening and for the story," he said, feeling a sense of gratitude and resolution.

The guardian nodded, his eyes reflecting a knowing kindness.

Chapter 6: Reunion

Their heartfelt conversation was abruptly cut short by the distant wail of police sirens, piercing the calm of the early morning. The serenity of the library was further shattered by the sudden flood of light as the doors swung open. In rushed Mike, his face a canvas of worry and relief. Without hesitation, he embraced James tightly, his actions speaking volumes of his fear and concern for the boy.

James, taken aback by the depth of emotion in Mike's reaction, felt a surge of surprise and understanding. Mike explained, breathless, that he had found James's library card near his folder at home and had guessed where he might be. The realization that Mike had been so concerned, had understood him so well, made something shift in James's perception.

As James turned to introduce the guardian to Mike, he noticed something astonishing. The old man, who had been so real and solid moments ago, was beginning to fade, his form becoming transparent before their eyes. Mike, looking around with a puzzled expression, mentioned that he couldn't see anyone.

In that surreal moment, James understood that the guardian was no ordinary man, but a spirit. As the guardian's form dissipated into the ether, he whispered to James, "You are my champion," a phrase that resonated deep within James's heart, a phrase only his father used to say.

For a brief moment, the guardian's face transformed, revealing the familiar, loving features of James's late father. It was a fleeting but profound revelation, leaving James with a sense of awe and comfort.

Tears welled up in James's eyes as he bid farewell to the guardian. His stepfather, overhearing the phrase "You are my champion," repeated it, his voice filled with emotion. He embraced James again, this time with a love that echoed his father's, a love that was genuine and deep.

It was a moment of profound realization for James – the understanding that while his father's physical presence was gone, his love and guidance continued to envelop him, a comforting and eternal presence.

This experience brought a new understanding and acceptance into James's heart. He began to see Mike not just as his stepfather but as someone who genuinely cared for him, someone who could help fill the void left by his father's absence. Not as a replacement, but as an additional source of love and support in his life.

As they walked home together under the starlit sky, a sense of peace settled over James. He knew that his journey of healing had just begun, but with Mike by his side, he felt equipped to face the challenges ahead. The love and memories of his father, like the guiding light of a guardian, would always be with him, in every step he took, every decision he made.

Together, under the vast, twinkling canopy of the night, they walked towards a future filled with hope, understanding, and the unbreakable bonds of family.

The Secret of the Story

Family can come in different forms, and we can find love and support from unexpected sources.

If you were in a disagreement with your parents, would you choose to talk it out or avoid the conversation? Why?

Zorlox's Pitch Galactic Games

Chapter 1: Welcome to Whimsyville!

In the tiny, slightly oddball town of Whimsyville, every day felt like a surprise waiting to happen. The town was a colorful patchwork of quirky shops, like 'Gloria's Glitter Emporium' and 'Bob's House of Bouncy Balls', and houses painted in every shade of the rainbow.

Right in the heart of this whimsical wonderland was Whimsyville Junior High, home to the most eclectic bunch of kids you'd ever meet. And then, of course, there were the Galactic Gophers, the school's junior baseball team, known more for their hilarious mishaps than their wins. But hey, they had spirit!

"Alright, team, let's show those Marauders what we're made of!" Coach Luna boomed, her voice echoing across the field. She was a peppy, middle-aged woman who wore sunglasses shaped like stars and believed in the power of pep talks and high-fives.

The team huddled around her, each member a character straight out of a comic book. Sammy 'Sticky Fingers' Thompson, known for catching things better than a spider web, joked, "Let's stick it to 'em!" Max 'The Whirlwind' Johnson, faster than a hiccup, quipped, "I'm so fast, I can run around the bases and high-five myself!" And Bella 'Boom Boom' Martinez, with a bat swing so powerful it could cause a mini earthquake, chuckled, "I hit home runs out of the park and into next week!"

The crowd began to gather, filling the stands with a sea of eager faces. Grandparents, parents, siblings, and a few curious squirrels (the unofficial mascots) were all there to cheer.

Just as the first pitch was about to be thrown, something extraordinary happened. A strange object zoomed across the sky, drawing everyone's eyes upwards. It wasn't a bird. It wasn't a plane. It was a... hot dog stand?

With a soft whoosh, the flying hot dog stand landed right in the outfield, kicking up a cloud of dust. The players and spectators stared in disbelief.

"Is this new advertising from a fast food?" whispered Max, scratching his head.

Chapter 2: Zorlox's Unexpected Arrival

The door creaked open, and out stepped Zorlox, a sight that would make any cartoon character jealous. Imagine a blueberry smoothie turned into a kid - that was Zorlox! His skin was a bright, glossy blue, shimmering as if he had just taken a dip in a galaxy far, far away. His arms were like those wacky, inflatable tube men you see at car dealerships, wiggling and jiggling in the most comical way. They stretched out longer than a Monday at school, making you wonder if they had an off switch.

His eyes were like two twinkling sapphires, wide with wonder and beaming with a mischievous sparkle that suggested he was ready for some extraterrestrial pranks. And his suit? Oh, it was like a disco ball met a chameleon. It changed colors with every move he made, flashing bright neon hues that would put the best Christmas lights to shame.

Zorlox stood there, a goofy grin plastered across his face, looking like he had just stepped out of the coolest sci-fi movie. The Galactic Gophers couldn't help but stare, their mouths hanging open wider than the Grand Canyon. Zorlox was not just an alien; he was the alien of the year, ready to bring a whole new level of fun to Whimsyville Junior High.

Chapter 3: Zorlox's Whimsical Whirlwind

In Whimsyville Junior High, the arrival of Zorlox, a blue-skinned, stretchy-armed alien, stirred up more excitement than a squirrel in a nut factory. The Galactic Gophers and the gathered crowd were buzzing with amazement at their newest, most unusual teammate.

"Whoa, he's bluer than a smurf on a cold day!" exclaimed Sammy, his eyes almost popping out. Zorlox, trying to understand, tilted his head and said, "Smurf? Is that an Earth creature? Can it play baseball too?"

Before anyone could answer, Bella, always the bold one, stepped up. "So, Zorlox, why did you beam down to our baseball field?" she asked, half-expecting him to say he was lost.

Zorlox blinked his big, sapphire eyes and replied with earnest confusion, "Beam down? Oh, no, I just parked my spaceship. I saw your game from the sky and thought, 'What a fun human ritual!'"

Max, the class clown, chuckled. "It's not a ritual, it's a game. And trust me, it's more fun than a monkey in a banana store!"

Zorlox looked puzzled, "Monkeys? Bananas? Your Earth words are very strange!"

Not everyone was amused by Zorlox's arrival. Jake, the team's star player, frowned from a distance. "An alien playing baseball? That's just weird," he muttered under his breath.

Coach Luna, always the peacemaker, decided it was time to introduce Zorlox to the game. "Baseball, Zorlox, is about hitting a ball, running around bases, and scoring runs. It's simple, but it's loads of fun!"

"Simple? But why do you run in a square? Why not a circle? Or a triangle?" Zorlox asked, genuinely baffled.

Sammy laughed. "Because running in circles would just make us dizzy!"

As Coach Luna explained the basics, Zorlox listened intently, occasionally scratching his head with his stretchy arm, which once accidentally wrapped around a nearby pole. "Oops, sorry! My arms are still learning Earth manners."

Zorlox tried swinging a bat, but instead of hitting the ball, he spun around, getting tangled in his own arms. "Maybe I should've read the manual on being an Earthling first!" he joked, trying to untangle himself.

The team couldn't help but laugh at Zorlox's antics. Even Jake, who had been skeptical, cracked a smile, though he quickly hid it.

Chapter 4: A Rocky Start for Zorlox

At the next practice, Coach Luna gathered the Galactic Gophers for an announcement. "Team, I've decided to give Zorlox a chance to play with us. Let's show him some team spirit!"

Zorlox, beaming with excitement, attempted a high-five but ended up stretching his arm too far, accidentally patting Sammy on the back... from ten feet away. "Oops, sorry! Still mastering Earthling high-fives," he chuckled.

Not everyone shared Coach Luna's enthusiasm. Jake, the team's star player, crossed his arms and rolled his eyes. "He doesn't even know how to high-five properly. How's he going to play baseball?"

Zorlox's first few practices were a mix of comedy and chaos. When Coach Luna explained the concept of a 'ball', Zorlox looked utterly perplexed. "You call it a ball, but it's not a party?" he asked, scratching his head with his stretchy arm.

Trying to teach Zorlox to bat was like teaching a cat to tap dance. He swung so wildly that he created a breeze, nearly sending Max's cap flying off. "Maybe aim for the ball, not the weather," Max suggested, dodging another enthusiastic swing.

Fielding was no less comical. Zorlox, excited to catch a fly ball, stretched his arms up, accidentally catching a bird instead. "Is this not the right kind of bird?" he asked, holding the confused bird gently before setting it free.

Despite the team's efforts, doubts began to creep in. "I'm not sure Zorlox is cut out for baseball," muttered Sammy during a water break. "He's more likely to catch a cloud than a ball."

Zorlox, overhearing, felt a pang of sadness but remained determined. "I will learn your Earth game," he said, trying to sound confident.

As the big game against the Meteorite Marauders approached, the team's anxiety grew. "We can't go into the game with a player who thinks a baseball is a party!" Jake complained.

Coach Luna, however, had a plan. "Let's give Zorlox a chance. You never know – he might surprise us all."

Chapter 5: Game Day Jitters

The morning of the big game against the Meteorite Marauders dawned bright and clear in Whimsyville. Excitement buzzed through the air like a swarm of hyperactive bees. The Galactic Gophers, their uniforms crisp and clean, were a bundle of nerves and excitement.

As the team gathered on the field, Zorlox bounced around, his stretchy arms accidentally flicking a baseball or two into the stands. "Is this part of the warm-up?" he asked, picking up another ball and juggling it with his wobbly arms.

Coach Luna, clipboard in hand, gave a pep talk. "Remember, it's not just about winning; it's about playing our best. And having fun!" She shot an encouraging smile at Zorlox, who was doing what could only be described as a 'pre-game alien dance'.

The crowd started filling the stands, a colorful sea of cheering fans. Whimsyville Junior High's mascot, a giant squirrel, danced around, adding to the festive atmosphere.

As the game kicked off, the Gophers took their positions. Zorlox, assigned to the outfield, waved enthusiastically to the crowd, nearly missing a fly ball. "I got it! I got it! Oops... almost got it!" he shouted, his arms stretching out just a second too late.

The Marauders were tough opponents, and it wasn't long before the Gophers started falling behind. Each missed catch and strikeout added to the team's growing anxiety. Sammy whispered to Max, "I hope we haven't bitten off more than we can chew with this game."

Meanwhile, Zorlox was having his own set of challenges. Every time a ball came his way, he either jumped too high, stretched too far, or got tangled up in his own limbs. "Earth gravity is trickier than I thought!" he exclaimed, trying to untangle himself after another missed catch.

Coach Luna watched from the sidelines, her expression a mix of concern and determination. The Gophers were struggling, and something needed to change, and fast.

Chapter 6: In a Pickle

As the innings progressed, the situation looked grim for the Galactic Gophers. The Marauders were racking up runs, and the Gophers' spirits were sinking faster than a lead balloon.

On the bench, the team's morale was low. Jake shook his head in frustration. "We're getting creamed out there. This is a disaster!"

Zorlox, his usual cheerful self, tried to lighten the mood. "On my planet, getting creamed means you're winning... in a pie-eating contest!" His joke earned a few weak smiles, but the stress of the game weighed heavily on the team.

In the outfield, Zorlox's attempts to catch the ball were met with more misses than hits. He leapt into the air, his arms stretching out like rubber bands, only to land in a clumsy heap, the ball bouncing away.

The crowd's cheers turned to murmurs of concern. Whispers spread through the stands, "Can the Gophers turn this around? Is Zorlox really helping?"

Coach Luna paced the dugout, deep in thought. She knew something had to be done, and she had an idea. But it was a gamble.

Chapter 7: Zorlox to the Rescue

By the seventh inning, the Gophers were trailing by five runs. Coach Luna took a deep breath and made a bold decision. "Zorlox, you're up to pitch!"

The team gasped. Zorlox's pitching was unpredictable at best. But Coach Luna's gut told her it was worth the risk.

Zorlox took the mound, his face a picture of concentration. His first pitch was a wild one, zooming over the batter's head and straight into the umpire's mitt. "Oops! Still calibrating!" he called out.

But as he continued, something miraculous happened. Zorlox's pitches, with their strange, stretchy-arm twists and turns, began to baffle the Marauders. One after another, they swung and missed.

The Gophers' energy reignited. Each strikeout by Zorlox fueled their comeback. Hits and runs started flowing, and the gap in the score began to close.

The final inning was a nail-biter. With the bases loaded, Zorlox delivered a pitch that zigzagged in the air like a lightning bolt. Strike three! The crowd erupted in cheers as the Gophers clinched the game in a spectacular turnaround.

Zorlox was hoisted onto his teammates' shoulders, the unlikely hero of the game.

Chapter 8: Hot Dogs and Farewells

After the incredible victory, Zorlox was the star of the hour. The entire field erupted into a celebration, with cheers and laughter echoing under the bright lights of the Whimsyville Junior High baseball field.

"Zorlox, you were out of this world today!" exclaimed Sammy, giving him a pat on the back.

"Yeah, sorry for doubting you," Jake said, sheepishly rubbing the back of his neck. "You pitched like a pro... a space pro!"

Zorlox beamed, his blue face glowing with happiness. "Thank you, Earth friends! You made me feel like I belong, even if I'm light-years away from home."

Just then, Zorlox's spaceship – still disguised as a hot dog stand – began to rumble. With a whoosh and a sizzle, it started churning out hot dogs in all directions. "Who wants Zorlox's Intergalactic Hot Dogs?" he announced, as the kids and spectators rushed towards the stand, laughing and cheering.

The hot dogs were like nothing they'd ever tasted – some were swirling with cosmic colors, others sparkled with edible stardust. "These hot dogs are literally out of this world!" Max said, munching on one that seemed to change flavors with every bite.

As the evening wore on, the field was filled with games and laughter. Zorlox, in the center of it all, felt a warmth in his heart. He had found friendship and joy in a place far from his home planet.

But as the stars twinkled overhead, Zorlox knew it was time to say goodbye. "My friends, I must return to Zibzob. I will teach my people this wonderful game of baseball and share the joy you've given me."

The team gathered around, their faces a mix of sadness and smiles. "You better come back, Zorlox. We'll need our star pitcher!" Bella said, trying to keep the mood light.

"Yes, I will return! And maybe next time, I'll bring my planet's version of baseball. Just a heads-up, it involves anti-gravity and moon rocks!"

The team laughed, imagining the chaos and fun that would bring. As Zorlox boarded his spaceship, he turned and waved. "Goodbye, my Earth friends! Keep playing and laughing!"

As the spaceship took off, leaving a trail of shimmering stardust in the sky, Sammy turned to the team and said, "Well, now we know what to do when we face the Marauders next year – just call for an alien pitcher!"

The team burst into laughter, the sound mingling with the distant hum of Zorlox's departing spaceship. The field was filled with a sense of adventure and anticipation for what the next season would bring, and maybe, just maybe, another visit from their friend from the stars.

The Secret of the Story

Embracing differences enriches your team, turning the unfamiliar into your greatest strength.

Imagine you have new friends who see the world in a special way and come from a place much different than yours. How would you make them feel welcome and help them enjoy being part of your group?

The Big Max

Chapter 1: A Gentle Giant's Beginnings

Max was a gentle giant, known for his warm and affectionate personality. His fur was a rich mix of browns and blacks, and his eyes sparkled with kindness.

Max's story began with a difficult start. It all happened during a chilly Christmas season, when the Greene family decided to surprise their children with a special gift. As they strolled through the town's bustling holiday market, they came across Max, a playful pup who immediately captured their hearts. Without a second thought, they decided to bring Max home as a surprise Christmas present for their two excited kids, Emily and Jake.

But as the days turned into weeks, the Greene family realized that taking care of a large and energetic Mastiff was not as easy as they had initially thought. Max's size, boundless energy, and enthusiasm for life were overwhelming for the family. They struggled to manage his needs and found themselves unprepared for the responsibility of caring for such a magnificent yet demanding dog.

As the holiday cheer faded away, so did the Greene family's enthusiasm for Max. The children lost interest in playing with him, and Max was left to spend most of his days alone in the backyard. He longed for companionship and love, but it seemed that the Greene family had given up on their impulsive Christmas gift.

One frigid winter day, Max found himself locked in a small kennel in the backyard, separated from the family he had once thought of as his own. The days turned into weeks, and Max's spirits dwindled. He missed the warmth of a loving home, the laughter of children, and the affectionate pats on the head. Max was a dog full of love, but he had been abandoned and left to wonder why.

As Max lay in his kennel, he could hear the Greene family's voices inside the house. They had seemingly moved on from their impulsive decision, but Max's heart remained heavy with sadness. He had known love, but it was a fleeting moment in his life, overshadowed by the difficulties that came with being a large and rambunctious puppy.

Eventually, the day came when the Greene family decided that Max was simply too much to handle, and they made the heart-wrenching decision to take him to a shelter and abandon him, showing little care for the gentle giant they had once welcomed into their home.

Chapter 2: Max's Arrival at the Williams Farm

Months passed by, and Max's days in the small kennel felt like an eternity. His once vibrant spirit had dimmed, and he yearned for a second chance at happiness. But Max's sheer size and the intimidating reputation of English Mastiffs made it difficult for him to find a new family.

Day after day, Max watched as potential adopters visited the shelter, their eyes widening in fear when they saw his massive frame and heard stories of his past. People assumed that he was too big and too scary, and they passed him by in search of smaller, friendlier dogs.

But just when it seemed that all hope was lost, a glimmer of light appeared on the horizon. A family by the name of Williams, who lived on a vast and picturesque farm on the outskirts of town, decided to pay a visit to the shelter. The Williams family had recently faced a burglary that left them shaken, and they were in need of a guard dog to protect their property.

As the Williams family walked through the rows of kennels, their eyes fell upon Max. He sat there, looking up at them with his gentle, soulful eyes, his massive paws and powerful physique hinting at his potential.

With a shared glance and a nod, they decided to adopt him.

As Max left the shelter and stepped into the world beyond, his heart raced with a mixture of hope and trepidation. The Williams family's farm stretched out before him like a sprawling canvas of natural beauty. It was unlike anything he had ever seen in his short life. Vast, rolling hills stretched as far as the eye could see, covered in lush green fields that swayed gently in the breeze. The centerpiece of this picturesque landscape was a magnificent big red barn, proudly standing tall against the horizon. Max's new home was a paradise for a dog like him, a place where he could run freely through the open fields and bask in the glory of nature's wonders.

Yet, amidst this breathtaking scenery, Max's excitement soon gave way to anxiety as he faced his first challenge in his new life – Buddy, the Williams family's older dog.

Chapter 3: Mr.Buddy

The sun was just beginning to set over the Williams' farm, painting the sky in shades of orange and purple as Max, the gentle giant of an English Mastiff, arrived at his new home. Eager and curious, Max stepped out of the truck, his bulky frame casting a long shadow on the ground. The farm was alive with new sights, sounds, and smells, all exciting to Max's keen senses.

Amid this new world, Max's eyes fell on Buddy, the farm's Border Collie. Buddy was no ordinary dog; he was the guardian of the farm, a position he held with pride. Despite his smaller size, Buddy was quick, intelligent, and fiercely protective. But lately, age had been catching up with him. His once sharp eyesight was dimming, and his reflexes, though still impressive, had slowed. This fact became painfully obvious during a recent burglary at the farm, where Buddy failed to hear the intruder, a mistake that weighed heavily on him.

Max, unaware of Buddy's internal struggles, approached him with a friendly wag. But Buddy's response was far from welcoming. He saw Max's size and perceived him as a potential rival, a threat to his long-held position as the farm's protector. With a low, warning growl, Buddy made it clear that he was still in charge.

Max, taken aback by this reception, retreated slightly. He couldn't understand why Buddy was so unwelcoming.

The Williams family observed this interaction with concern. They knew Buddy's time as the sole guardian of the farm was coming to an end, and they hoped he would accept Max as a companion, maybe even as a successor. But Buddy's growls and guarded stance showed that this transition wouldn't be easy.

That night, as Max settled into his new bed in the barn, he thought about his new life and about Buddy. He wondered if they could ever get along.

Meanwhile, Buddy lay on the porch, his eyes fixed on the barn. He felt a pang of fear and insecurity. Max was younger, stronger, and even in his brief time at the farm, he had shown a natural gentleness that endeared him to the Williams family. Buddy knew deep down that Max wasn't a threat, but he couldn't shake the feeling that his time as the top dog might be coming to an end.

Chapter 4: Adjusting to New Challenges

In the heart of the Williams' farm, under the watchful gaze of the early morning sun, Max began another day, filled with the hope of fitting into his new home. However, the reality was far from easy. Buddy, the farm's seasoned protector, continued to view Max with distrust and hostility, his growls a constant reminder of the welcome he wasn't receiving.

Max, with his towering frame and gentle eyes, tried to approach the farm animals and explore his surroundings, but Buddy's watchful presence cast a shadow over his attempts. The other animals, taking cues from Buddy, remained distant, leaving Max to wander the fields alone, his heart heavy with loneliness.

Meanwhile, the Williams family watched with growing disappointment. They had hoped Max would take on the role of a guard dog, a role that Buddy was slowly outgrowing. But Max's temperament, though endearing, lacked the aggression they expected. His gentle nature, while a blessing in many ways, did not fit the mold of the traditional guard dog they had in mind.

One evening, Mr. Williams sat on the porch, watching Max amble across the yard. "He's just not what we thought he'd be," he said, a hint of regret in his voice. Mrs. Williams, always the optimist, suggested they give Max more time to adjust, to find his place in their world.

Chapter 5: Max's Decision

That evening, as the stray cat stealthily approached the chicken coop, causing a slight commotion, Max's reaction, or lack thereof, puzzled the Williams family. They watched from the window, expecting him to charge towards the disturbance as any guard dog would. But Max, despite his size and strength, remained still, his gaze fixed on the darkened edge of the farm.

Max, with his keen sense of smell, had indeed noticed the cat. However, his instincts told him that this small creature posed no real threat to the farm. Unlike Buddy, who would have barked and chased it away, Max assessed the situation differently. In his calm and thoughtful demeanor, Max understood that not every unfamiliar presence was a danger. The cat was merely a curious visitor, not a predator or a thief.

Mr. Williams, from the other side of the room, observing this, let out a sigh, a mix of frustration and disbelief coloring his voice. "He's just not cut out for this," he said, reflecting on Max's apparent lack of aggression. This was not the guard dog behavior they had envisioned when they welcomed Max into their home.

This moment underscored the stark contrast between Max and Buddy, and the challenge Max faced in meeting the family's expectations. His gentle nature, so at odds with the traditional guard dog persona, left the Williams family wondering if he could ever fulfill the role, they had envisioned for him.

Chapter 6: Max's Heroic Night

As the days passed on the Williams' farm, Max's presence became a quiet backdrop to the daily routines. His gentle nature and lack of traditional guard dog aggression continued to disappoint the Williams family. They began to doubt their decision, considering the possibility of returning Max to the shelter. Max, sensing their disappointment, grew increasingly despondent, longing to prove his worth.

Then, one fateful night, everything changed. As the farm slept, a small fire sparked in the barn, its flames slowly growing, threatening to engulf the structure. Max, awakened by the scent of smoke, immediately sensed the danger. His heart raced, not with fear, but with a determined resolve. He knew Buddy, his unlikely companion, was sleeping inside the barn.

Without hesitation, Max dashed towards the burning barn, his powerful frame cutting through the night. Inside, he found Buddy, disoriented and scared amidst the growing flames. With a nudge of his nose, Max urged Buddy to follow him out of the barn. Once Buddy was safe, Max knew he had to alert the family. He raced to the house, barking loudly, a sound so urgent and unfamiliar that it roused the Williams family from their deep sleep.

But Max didn't stop there. His instincts led him to the nearby water hose. With his mouth, he turned on the tap, allowing water to flow towards the flames. It was a small act, but it bought precious time.

The Williams family, now fully awake, rushed to the scene, their hearts pounding with fear and confusion. As they arrived, they saw Max, standing bravely near the barn, his coat singed by the heat. The sight of Max, not only saving Buddy but also taking steps to control the fire, filled them with awe.

The firefighters arrived soon after, extinguishing the remaining flames. The barn was damaged, but thanks to Max's quick actions, the fire had not spread, and no lives were lost. As the sun rose over a smoke-scented farm, the Williams family looked at Max with newfound respect and gratitude. His heroism had not only saved Buddy's life but also changed their perception of him forever. Max, once seen as a disappointment, had proven to be a true guardian, his bravery and quick thinking overshadowing any previous doubts about his role on the farm.

Chapter 7: A New Beginning

In the golden morning light, the Williams family encircled Max, their faces etched with emotions of awe, love, and a deep sense of regret. The heroism Max displayed the night before had opened their eyes to the extraordinary soul that resided in their gentle giant – not merely as a conventional guard dog, but as a brave, intelligent companion with a heart full of loyalty. They deeply regretted ever considering returning him to the shelter and promised to embrace him for who he truly was. Their preconceived notions of what a guard dog should be had blinded them to Max's unique qualities. They embraced him, showering him with hugs and kisses, their apologies whispered into his soft fur. Each member of the family took a moment to express their gratitude and love, vowing never again to underestimate him.

Buddy, observing this heartfelt scene, approached Max with a new sense of respect. He remembered the fear and confusion of the fire and how Max had fearlessly saved him. The realization dawned on Buddy that he had misjudged Max, mistreated him even, when all along, Max was a loyal friend. With a soft nuzzle, a gesture uncharacteristic of the usually stoic Buddy, he acknowledged Max's bravery and accepted him as a genuine member of the family.

The farm, once a place of uncertainty for Max, transformed into a home where he was cherished for his unique qualities. The bond between Max and the Williams family deepened, rooted in mutual respect, and understanding. Max and Buddy, now brothers in spirit, patrolled the farm together, a testament to the unbreakable bond formed under extraordinary circumstances.

As the chapter closes, we see the Williams family, Max, and Buddy, sitting together, watching the sun cast its warm hues over the farm. Laughter and barks fill the air, symbolizing a new beginning. Max, once an outsider, had not only found his forever home but had also taught everyone the true meaning of courage, unconditional love, and the irreplaceable value of accepting others for who they truly are.

The Secret of the Story

True heroism lies not in how we look but in the bravery of our actions and the kindness of our hearts.

Have you ever changed your mind about someone after getting to know them, realizing they were quite different from what you first thought based on their appearance?

Crispy and the Oceaneaters

Chapter 1: The Colorful World of the Coral Reef

Beneath the sparkling surface of the ocean, where the sun's rays painted rainbows in the water, lay a coral reef bursting with life.

Crispy the crab and Finny the fish were engaged in a lively game of tag. Crispy, with his vibrant blue shell and distinctive yellow tuft, dodged and weaved with agility, while Finny, bright red and quick as a flash, darted after him. Their laughter echoed through the water, full of life and joy.

As they played, they came close to colliding with Annie the anemone. Her tentacles, a beautiful array of colors, swayed gracefully in the water, almost like a slow dance. Just as the two friends neared her, Otto the octopus intervened with a swift movement of his tentacle, catching a stray pebble that would have hit Annie. His intelligent eyes sparkled with amusement, his tentacles moving with a skillful grace that spoke of his deep understanding of their underwater world.

The game resumed with renewed vigor, but soon, a large shadow loomed over them – it was Sam the shark. For a moment, fear gripped the reef as Sam's large figure approached. His sleek, powerful form and the scar above his eye, a remnant of a past encounter, made him an imposing figure. But as he drew closer, his demeanor softened, revealing a gentleness unexpected of a shark. Crispy had once bravely freed Sam from a fisherman's net, an act that had transformed fear into friendship.

As the sun began to set on the coral reef, casting a golden glow over its inhabitants, the day's adventures drew to a close. Crispy, Finny, Otto, Annie, and even Sam the shark, each returned to their chosen nooks of the reef. Their world was one of endless wonder, a place where each day was filled with laughter and playful escapades. But beneath the surface of these joyful moments, there was an unspoken understanding that the ocean also held its dangers.

Chapter 2: The Threat of the Oceaneaters

A new day began in the reef, the water shimmering with the morning light. Everything seemed peaceful until a sudden cry echoed through the water.

"Oceaneaters! Oceaneaters!"

"Swim, swim!"

Panic spread as the current launched thousands of colorful glitters through the reef, resembling a storm of tiny, menacing invaders.

The fish cried out in alarm, and all the reef dwellers rushed to find shelter.

In the safety of their cave, Crispy and his friends huddled together. The reef, usually a place of joy and adventure, now felt threatened by these mysterious Oceaneaters. As they waited for the danger to pass, the group began to share their experiences and knowledge about these enigmatic entities.

Otto's voice, laced with concern, narrated the tale of Oceaneaters, shapeshifting entities that could blend seamlessly into the ocean's vast expanse, posing an invisible yet ever-present danger. He recounted the story of Jellymarie, a graceful jellyfish, who had succumbed to the cunning deception of an Oceaneater. Floating serenely in Sirenea Park, Jellymarie encountered a deceitful predator, perfectly mimicking the jellyfish's graceful motion. Unraveling its disguise too late, Jellymarie was enveloped by the Oceaneater, vanishing into thin air, leaving behind only whispers of her tragic fate.

Annie added that these creatures were not just mere illusions; they were real and could cause severe harm if one wasn't careful.

Her voice trembling with fear, recounted the harrowing tale of Rully the dolphin, who had become an unsuspecting victim of an Oceaneater's deceptive disguise. As Rully was playfully chasing what he thought was a harmless fish, the Oceaneater's true nature was revealed when Rully swallowed it, unleashing a torrent of excruciating pain. Rully's screams echoed through the ocean, sending shivers down the spines of his companions.

His anguished cries reached the ears of the esteemed pufferfish doctor, Puff, who embarked on a delicate operation to extract the Oceaneater from

Rully's throat. Puff maneuvered his beak through Rully's constricted airways, and finally emerged holding the Oceaneater aloft. Rully, weakened but alive, was carried back to his pod.

Sam, with a serious tone, recounted his own encounters with the Oceaneaters. He had seen them transform into various shapes, blending perfectly with the ocean surroundings, making it almost impossible to detect them until it was too late.

These stories, shared in the dim light of their underwater sanctuary, served as a grim reminder of the cunning and danger posed by the Oceaneaters. They were not merely camouflaged threats but could inflict physical harm.

As the group cautiously left their refuge, Crispy, with a serious expression, voiced a troubling observation. "Once, Oceaneaters were a rare sight in our reef, but now, they appear almost every day. They are growing in numbers, and each of us must be vigilant." He looked around at his friends, his eyes conveying the urgency of the situation. "Remember, if you spot one, swim away as fast as you can!"

Chapter 3: Crispy's Ordeal in the Storm

The day had started like any other in the reef, but as the afternoon wore on, the sky darkened ominously. A storm was brewing, one that seemed fiercer than any Crispy had ever witnessed. The once gentle currents turned wild and unpredictable, thrashing about with untamed ferocity.

Crispy, caught in the midst of this aquatic turmoil, fought valiantly against the currents that threatened to sweep him away from his home. But nature's force proved too strong. The currents carried him further into the depths of the ocean, into territories unknown and frightening.

Amidst the swirling waters, a sinister shape emerged. It was an Oceaneater, transparent and almost ethereal, blending seamlessly with the water. Crispy, with his keen eyes, spotted it at the very last second, but his efforts to evade were in vain. The Oceaneater's presence was like a silent predator, waiting for the perfect moment to strike.

In an instant, the Oceaneater enveloped Crispy, sucking him into its formless body. The world outside became a blur as he passed through the narrow maw of the creature. Inside, the Oceaneater's belly was like a transparent chamber, a window to the ocean he could no longer touch. Crispy was trapped, his movements restricted by the tight space.

He could see the storm raging outside, the flashes of lightning illuminating the sea in brief, stark glimpses. The sounds of the tempest were muffled, leaving Crispy in a surreal silence. It was a haunting experience, being able to see his world but being cut off from it completely.

As the storm raged on, Crispy's thoughts turned to his friends. Would they be searching for him? Could they even guess where the currents had taken him? The feeling of isolation was overwhelming, a stark contrast to the lively community of the reef he was so accustomed to.

Crispy's situation seemed dire. The Oceaneater's mouth, the very passage through which he had been sucked in, was far too narrow to consider as an escape route. The realization hit him hard – escaping on his own was impossible. He was at the mercy of the sea and the whims of the Oceaneater.

As the hours passed, the storm began to subside, but Crispy remained a prisoner within the Oceaneater. His hope of returning to the reef, to his friends and the life he cherished, seemed to fade with each passing moment. The adventure he had always sought had turned into a nightmare, one from which he desperately hoped to awake.

Chapter 4: Crispy's Unexpected Rescue

Hours passed, and inside the Oceaneater, Crispy felt a sense of hopelessness. He had resigned himself to his fate after being engulfed by the Oceaneaters, thinking it was the end of his underwater adventures. However, to his surprise, nothing had happened. The sea gradually calmed down, and the Oceaneaters decided to surface.

Just at that moment, a group of fishermen aboard a weathered fishing boat was in the midst of pulling up their heavy nets. Unbeknownst to them, the Oceaneaters, invisible beneath the water's surface, became entangled in the fishermen's catch.

Crispy watched in disbelief as the net was hoisted onto the deck of the boat. He saw everything that unfolded but was powerless to do anything, trapped within the Oceaneater. His thoughts raced as he realized that he had gone from one dire situation to another. "From the frying pan to the grill," he thought wryly, acknowledging the irony of his predicament.

Tom, the fisherman, began to assess their haul, counting the fish that had been caught. As he surveyed the tangled net, he noticed something peculiar—a plastic bottle was ensnared among the catch. At first, he considered tossing it back into the sea without much interest.

However, as he held the bottle up to examine it more closely, Tom noticed movement inside. He squinted, his curiosity piqued, and to his astonishment, he saw a colorful crab with a distinctive yellow tuft trapped within the bottle.

"Hey there, little guy," Tom exclaimed with a smile, addressing the crab inside the bottle. "What are you doing inside this bottle? You look funny with that yellow tuft. I might just take you to Lily; I'm sure she'll like you."

With gentle hands, Tom carefully removed the plastic bottle from the net, being mindful of the crab within. He marveled at the unexpected discovery and decided to take Crispy home with him.

Crispy, still bewildered by the sudden turn of events, couldn't help but wonder what lay ahead in this new chapter of his underwater journey. As

Tom placed the bottle containing Crispy on the deck of the fishing boat, the crab felt a glimmer of hope.

Chapter 5: Lily's Aquarium

Crispy's journey had taken an unexpected turn as he found himself at the fisherman's house. At his home, Tom retrieved a sharp knife from his fishing gear.

Crispy held his breath as he saw him approaching him and the Oceaneater.

Gently and methodically, Tom cut away the plastic bottle, ensuring not to harm Crispy in the process.

Then, he placed Crispy in a small aquarium and made his way to his daughter's room. The room itself paid homage to the sea, adorned with posters depicting underwater landscapes and shelves brimming with a colorful assortment of sea toys. It was evident that Lily had a deep love for the ocean, and the room beautifully reflected her passion.

"Lily," he said, his voice filled with excitement, "I have something special to show you."

Lily's eyes widened with curiosity as she rushed over to her father. She peered into the aquarium and saw Crispy, the colorful crab with the distinctive yellow tuft, swimming gracefully in the seawater. Her face lit up with delight as she observed the crab's vibrant presence.

"Daddy, he's beautiful!" Lily exclaimed; her enthusiasm contagious.

Crispy appreciated that comment; even humans found him charming.

He couldn't help but feel a sense of awe as he observed Lily. She was a young girl with bright, curious eyes that sparkled with fascination. Lily had a gentle and caring demeanor, and she took an immediate interest in her new aquatic guest. She approached the aquarium with a sense of wonder, her small hand gently pressing against the glass.

Chapter 6: Crispy's Yearning

As the days stretched into weeks, Crispy's existence within the confines of the aquarium grew increasingly challenging. Despite Lily's best efforts to create a welcoming and vibrant environment, the crab couldn't shake the persistent sense of isolation that gnawed at him.

Lily's voice was like a soothing melody to Crispy's ears as she spoke to him in soft, unintelligible murmurs. She would spend hours in her room, sitting by the aquarium and watching Crispy's every move. Her attempts to engage with the crab were evident as she would playfully tap the glass, trying to get his attention.

However, the longing for his oceanic world, once teeming with vibrant life and the laughter of his friends, weighed heavily on his soul.

Crispy had transformed from the lively and colorful crab of his reef into a symbol of profound longing and solitude. The posters of the sea that adorned Lily's room were his only connection to the world he had left behind, and he would gaze at them wistfully, hoping to catch a fleeting reminder of his true home.

Lily, who had initially been excited about her new "pet," began to notice the sadness of his friend. With unwavering determination, Lily set out to make Crispy's life in the aquarium more enjoyable. She added colorful decorations and an array of sea-themed toys, hoping to lift the crab's spirits. She even danced and twirled around the room in an attempt to entertain him, thinking her youthful exuberance might bring some joy to Crispy's life.

But despite her efforts, Crispy's sadness remained unabated.

Chapter 7: Return to the Ocean

As time passed, a sudden and drastic change overcame Crispy. His once-bright blue colors began to fade rapidly, and the distinctive tuft atop his shell turned a haunting shade of grey.

Lily watched in growing alarm as her dear crab friend's transformation unfolded before her eyes. The sight filled her with fear, and she couldn't bear to see Crispy's health deteriorate any further.

Lily made a decision. She realized that her beloved pet was yearning for his natural environment, the vast and vibrant ocean he had once called home. She knew what she had to do.

Approaching her father with determination, Lily said, "Daddy, I think Crispy is unhappy here. He misses the ocean. We should return him."

Her father, understanding the depth of Lily's love for the crab, agreed without hesitation. Together, they made the necessary preparations for Crispy's return to the sea.

On the day of Crispy's release, Lily and her father accompanied him to the shore. Crispy, sensing the familiar scent of the ocean, tapped his claws with excitement against the sides of the container. Lily carefully released him into the gentle waves, and he eagerly disappeared beneath the water's surface.

As they prepared to bid Crispy farewell, he surprised them with a gesture of affection and gratitude. With one of his claws, he playfully sprayed water in Lily's direction, causing her to laugh and feel deeply touched by the crab's appreciation.

Once back in the ocean, Crispy underwent a remarkable transformation. His colors began to return, and his tuft once again turned a brilliant shade of yellow. With boundless joy, he reunited with his friends from the coral reef, regaling them with humorous tales of his "adventures" in the aquarium.

Lily and her father, profoundly moved by their experience with Crispy, made a heartfelt commitment to help protect the ocean and its precious inhabitants. They decided to start picking up plastic debris on the beach to prevent other marine creatures from suffering the same fate that had befallen Crispy.

As Crispy thrived in his renewed life in the ocean, he knew that his time with Lily had been a unique and treasured chapter in his underwater journey. It was a story of friendship, understanding, and the enduring bond between a young girl and a colorful crab, a story that would be treasured by both sea and shore.

The Secret of the Story

Every creature has its rightful place in the environment and happiness truly lies in living in harmony with nature.

How can we help protect the ocean and its creatures, and why is it important to keep animals in their natural habitat?

The Glowing Trees of Valle Dorada

Chapter 1: The Mysterious Light

In Valle Dorada, a small village nestled among green hills, lived Ethan, a boy no older than twelve. His clothes were a bit too big for him, and his sneakers had seen better days. Every day, Ethan searched for food, his stomach often grumbling louder than the thunder on a rainy day.

One evening, with his pockets as empty as his belly, Ethan made a brave decision. He would venture into the mysterious forest, a place where shadows danced and the unknown lurked. "What if I meet a wolf?" he thought, a shiver running down his spine. But his hunger pushed him forward.

As the sky turned orange and pink, Ethan stepped into the forest. The trees were like giant guardians, and the air smelled like adventure. Suddenly, he saw something strange—a glowing light bouncing between the trees! "Wow, is that a firefly party?" Ethan wondered, forgetting his fears.

Curious, he followed the light. It felt like a game of hide and seek, with the light always just a step ahead. Finally, the light led him to a secret pond, where the water was as clear as glass. Hovering above the pond was a fairy, shining like a star!

Ethan rubbed his eyes. "Am I dreaming?" he whispered. The fairy smiled and said, "I'm real, Ethan. And I have a gift for you." She handed him three glowing seeds. "These are special," she said. "If you care for them with love, they'll give you food. But be careful, they hold a secret!"

Ethan's heart raced with excitement. "A secret? What could it be?" He thanked the fairy and ran home, the seeds safe in his pocket.

Chapter 2: The Magic Begins

Ethan planted the seeds in a small patch of dirt near his home. "Grow well, little seeds," he said, watering them with care. He even sang to them, thinking it might help.

To his surprise, the seeds sprouted overnight! "Whoa, that was fast!" Ethan exclaimed. The plants grew taller each day, and Ethan felt like a proud parent.

One night, Ethan woke up to a soft glow outside his window. The plants had grown into tall trees, and they were covered in fruits that shone like tiny moons. "This is amazing!" Ethan laughed, dancing under the glowing trees.

When the fruits ripened, glowing like jewels under the moonlit sky, Ethan felt a thrill unlike any other. He picked the first fruit, its light warm in his hands. The taste was heavenly, a burst of flavors he had never known. "This is incredible!" he thought, his heart swelling with joy.

Eager to share his newfound joy, Ethan invited his neighbors to taste the fruits from his magical trees. "Here, try these! They're from my special trees," he said, his voice tinged with a rare pride. As they bit into the fruits, their faces lit up with delight, the glowing light painting their expressions with wonder. The neighbors were amazed and deeply grateful, showering Ethan with praises for his extraordinary trees.

But word of the magical orchard spread like wildfire through Valle Dorada. Before long, not just neighbors, but people from all corners of the village and beyond started arriving. Each night, Ethan's orchard transformed into a spectacle of shimmering lights, as more trees grew, each aglow with fruits that shone brighter than the last. It was like a festival of stars on earth, with the trees' radiant dance captivating everyone who saw it.

Initially, Ethan felt a swell of happiness seeing others enjoy the beauty of his trees. They laughed and played under the glowing branches, and some even took a fruit or two. But as the crowds grew larger, the fear of losing everything became overwhelming. "What if they take all the fruits?" he thought. His heart, once full of joy, now felt a pinch of fear.

Ethan's worry about his special place grew stronger and stronger, like a prickly vine wrapping itself around his heart.

Driven by a growing sense of protectiveness and a desire to reclaim his space, Ethan decided to build a wall. Not just any wall, but a towering structure, so high that it seemed to reach for the clouds. He spent days stacking bricks and stones, his hands working tirelessly. The wall was formidable, with its rough surface casting a large shadow both literally and metaphorically over the orchard.

Once completed, the wall stood as a barrier between Ethan and the world. It loomed over the once welcoming orchard, turning it into a secluded fortress. The glowing fruits were finally hidden from strangers' view.

Chapter 3: The Lonely Guardian

In the quiet days that followed, Ethan stood watch over his glowing orchard, now shrouded behind the tall, imposing wall. Every night, he patrolled the perimeter, ensuring that no one came close. The wall, meant to be a shield, gradually became a cage that not only kept others out but also trapped Ethan in his loneliness.

Ethan's world had shrunk to the confines of his orchard. His every thought was about protecting the glowing fruits that had become his obsession. He saw every outsider as a potential thief, someone who might strip away the one good thing that had happened to him. "These trees are mine, and mine alone," he thought, his young face often creased with worry.

One day, as the sun dipped below the horizon, Ethan heard a rustling near the wall. Peering through a small gap, he saw Maggie, a girl from the village, trying to catch a glimpse of the once-famous glowing trees.

"Go away! You can't be here!" Ethan shouted.

Maggie, startled and hurt, ran away.

The villagers, who once looked at him with admiration, now saw him as a hoarder of joy, a keeper of beauty that he refused to share. Their visits stopped, and the laughter and chatter that once filled the air around the orchard were replaced by silence.

In the following days, Ethan often saw a shadow approaching his orchard. He could swear it was that girl, who continued to disturb him.

Chapter 4: Fading Lights

As the nights passed, Ethan noticed another change—a wilting in the trees, a dimming of their light. The fruits, once vibrant and full of life, now hung heavily, their glow fading. Panic gripped Ethan. "What's happening to them?" he wondered, a sinking feeling in his stomach.

As days turned into weeks, the once vibrant orchard of Valle Dorada, hidden behind Ethan's towering wall, grew dimmer. The trees, laden with fewer fruits, cast only a feeble glow, a mere shadow of their former splendor. Ethan's heart was heavy with despair. He wandered amidst the fading trees, feeling lost and alone, wondering if the fairy's gift was indeed a curse in disguise.

One evening, as Ethan sat under the gloomiest tree, lost in his thoughts of regret, he heard a gentle voice calling his name. It was Maggie, standing just outside the wall, her face lit by the soft moonlight. Ethan, surprised and cautious, approached the wall reluctantly.

"How did you find me here?" he asked, his voice barely above a whisper.

"I've been watching the orchard," Maggie replied, her eyes reflecting sincere concern. "I saw how the lights dimmed, and I knew something was wrong. I wanted to help, Ethan. Maybe together we can figure out what's happening."

Ethan hesitated, his instinct to protect the orchard battling with the growing sense of desperation. Finally, his loneliness and worry overcame his reluctance. He unlocked the gate and let Maggie in.

Together, they walked through the orchard, their footsteps soft on the grassy ground. The air was filled with a palpable sadness, as if the trees themselves were mourning their lost brilliance.

As they reached the heart of the orchard, Maggie pointed towards a large tree, where a single fruit hung, emitting a faint glow. "Look, Ethan," she said softly. "This one still has some light. Maybe there's hope."

Ethan's eyes widened as he saw the tiny glowing fruit. It was the only spark of light in the entire orchard, a fragile beacon in the darkness. Something about it seemed different, almost hopeful.

Ethan and Maggie spent several nights sitting under the tree, watching the small glowing fruit with bated breath. Each evening, the glow of the fruit grew stronger, its light a little more confident. They talked quietly as they waited, their words floating up into the branches. Maggie shared stories from the village, while Ethan, slowly shedding his protective shell, talked about his dreams and fears.

As they returned night after night, they noticed other tiny fruits beginning to emerge, each emitting its own faint glow. It was as if the first fruit's light was encouraging the others to shine. Together, they nurtured these new fruits, and soon, they too ripened, casting a warm, inviting glow across the orchard.

During these nights, a friendship blossomed between Ethan and Maggie. Ethan found comfort in Maggie's presence, her optimism and kindness breaking through the walls he had built around himself. He began to laugh more, his laughter mingling with the soft luminescence of the trees. The fear and loneliness that had once consumed him started to fade away, replaced by a newfound sense of hope and connection.

As Ethan and Maggie observed the few glowing trees in the orchard, they realized they needed more insights to fully restore the orchard's magic. Maggie came up with an idea. "Ethan, what if we invite the whole village to see the trees? They might help too," she suggested one night, her eyes sparkling with excitement.

Ethan was hesitant at first. The thought of inviting the villagers, whom he had shut out, back into his orchard stirred a mix of emotions within him.

"Okay, let's do it," Ethan agreed, a nervous yet hopeful smile crossing his face. "But do you think they'll come, after everything?"

Maggie's smile was reassuring. "They will, Ethan. They miss the orchard too."

Chapter 5: The Village's Return

Together, they spread the word throughout Valle Dorada, inviting every-one to Ethan's orchard. His heart pounded with anticipation and a bit of fear as the day approached. He had no idea how the villagers would react.

The villagers, initially reluctant due to past grievances with Ethan, were eventually moved by his genuine plea for assistance. Slowly, they started to gather in the orchard each evening, intrigued by the mystery of the fading lights and motivated by a desire to help. They shared ideas, tried different approaches to nurture the trees.

As days passed, more and more people from Valle Dorada joined the nightly gatherings. As the evening approached, Valle Dorada witnessed an extraordinary sight. An army of villagers descended upon the orchard, their collective energy radiating through the trees. Their presence, initially motivated by curiosity and a shared desire to help, soon transformed into a collective effort to revive the orchard's magic.

Ethan and Maggie watched, hearts pounding, as the villagers filled the once-lonely orchard. Then, a miraculous event unfolded: thousands of fireflies began to swarm the orchard, their lights weaving a mesmerizing dance in the twilight. But upon closer inspection, Ethan realized they weren't fireflies at all – they were tiny, glowing fruits sprouting on the trees!

Ethan's eyes widened in disbelief as the orchard slowly came back to life. The trees, once dim and forlorn, now shone with vibrant lights, their branches heavy with glowing fruits. The air was filled with exclamations of wonder and joy from the villagers, their smiles illuminating the night.

Overwhelmed with emotion, Ethan turned to embrace Maggie, wanting to share this triumphant moment with her. But to his surprise, she was nowhere to be found.

Chapter 6: The Secret Revealed

As the jubilant celebrations unfolded over several days in Valle Dorada, the orchard became a beacon of joy and community spirit. Families, friends, and neighbors gathered under the glowing canopy, their laughter and chatter creating a festive atmosphere.

During one such evening, a timid boy, his eyes wide with wonder, approached Ethan. He reminded Ethan of himself in earlier days - a child familiar with want and need. "Can I take one of these fruits for my brothers and sisters at home?" the boy asked in a hesitant whisper.

Ethan's heart swelled with empathy. He remembered his own struggles and how much this gesture would have meant to him. He addressed the crowd, his voice clear and resonant, "Everyone, take what you need from the orchard. These fruits are for all of us, thanks to your help in saving them. They exist because of your kindness and joy."

As these words left Ethan's lips, he heard Maggie's voice, "Well done, Ethan. You've solved the mystery!" But when he turned around, Maggie was not there. Instead, standing before him was the fairy from the pond, her smile gentle and wise. She revealed herself as the one who had been with him in Maggie's guise, guiding him to understand the true nature of the orchard.

The fairy explained that the magic of the fruits was fueled by the good intentions and collective joy of those who nurtured and admired them. The orchard was a reflection of the community's heart, thriving on shared care and happiness.

Ethan, moved by this revelation, promised himself and the fairy that he would always share everything he had. The fairy, pleased with Ethan's growth and understanding, hovered gracefully in the air, her light mingling with the vibrant glow of the orchard.

As she ascended into the night, leaving behind a trail of luminous sparkles, Ethan stood amidst his fellow villagers, a sense of fulfillment and unity filling his heart. The orchard, now a symbol of shared prosperity and community bond, continued to glow brightly, a testament to the enduring magic of generosity and collaboration in Valle Dorada.

The Secret of the Story

True joy and magic grow not from keeping treasures to ourselves but from sharing them with those around us.

What would you do if you found something special that everyone wanted? Would you keep it to yourself or share it with others?

The Saga of the Dragons of Drakonia

Chapter 1: The Valley of Laziness

In the mystical land of Drakonia, hidden among towering mountains, there lay a forgotten valley known as the Valley of the Winds. This valley, shrouded in mist and magic, was home to a unique tribe of dragons. Among them were three young dragons: Ember, a fiery red dragon; Zephyr, a swift blue dragon; and Terra, a sturdy earth-colored dragon.

Life in the Valley of the Winds was peaceful but uneventful. The dragons, once known for their majesty and power, had grown accustomed to a life of comfort and ease. They spent their days lounging in the sun, munching on plump, juicy fruits, and telling tales of the old days when dragons ruled the skies.

Ember, Zephyr, and Terra were no different. They had never known the thrill of soaring through the clouds or feeling the wind rushing past their scales.

Ember, with his striking red scales that sparkled in the sunlight, often found himself gazing wistfully at the vast expanse above. His heart harbored dreams of soaring through the heavens, but his thin, frail wings, untested and weak, were a constant reminder of the sedentary life he led.

Zephyr, his scales a soothing shade of blue, echoed the calm of the clear skies he had never touched. A dragon of few words, Zephyr spent hours lounging by the babbling brooks, his mind adrift in thoughts as serene as his demeanor. His well-rounded figure spoke volumes of the languid lifestyle in the valley, where action was often replaced by contemplation.

Terra, the most grounded of the trio, bore earth-toned scales that blended seamlessly with the nature around her. Though she was the smallest, her sturdy build and determined eyes showed a hidden resilience. Like her friends, Terra's wings were stunted, a testament to generations of grounded living.

The days in the Valley of Winds were unhurried and peaceful. Dragons of all ages lounged under the shade of giant ferns, their days filled with napping, feasting on an abundance of fruits, and leisurely conversations that meandered like the lazy rivers around them. The art of flying, once a symbol of their kind's majesty, had become a tale of folklore, retold but never relived.

Young dragons like Ember, Zephyr, and Terra grew up listening to these tales, their imaginations painting vibrant pictures of the sky, a realm they had never explored. Yet, the comfort of their daily routine, the easy access to food, and the safety of the valley's embrace had lulled them into complacency.

In this paradise of idleness, ambitions were as fleeting as the morning dew, and dreams of flight were as distant as the stars twinkling in the night sky. The Valley of Winds, with its beauty and tranquility, held the dragons in a gentle, unyielding grip, its lullaby convincing them that the ground was enough, and the heavens were just a dream too far.

The art of flying had become a mere legend, a relic of a past that the young dragons could hardly imagine.

Each day was much like the last in the Valley of Laziness, as the dragons fondly called it. The elders would reminisce about the days of yore, while the younglings would dream of adventures they never dared to embark upon.

But Ember was different. He often gazed up at the sky, his heart aching with a desire for something more, something beyond the lazy routine of the valley. He longed to feel the rush of air under his wings, to explore the vast world beyond the mountains that encircled their home.

One day, as Ember lay on a sun-soaked rock, he shared his restlessness with Zephyr and Terra. "Don't you ever wonder what it's like to fly? To truly fly?" he asked, his eyes sparkling with a barely contained passion.

Zephyr shrugged, his blue scales glinting in the sunlight. "Maybe, but flying is just an old dragon's tale. We're fine just the way we are."

Terra nodded in agreement, her earthy scales blending in with the rocks around them. "Why bother with the effort? The ground is good enough for me."

Chapter 2: Solara's Wisdom

As the days passed in the Valley of Winds, Ember's sense of restlessness grew. Watching his fellow dragons laze about day after day, with no ambition beyond the next meal or nap, stirred a deep frustration within him. He longed for more than just stories of the past; he yearned to live those adventures himself.

One particularly bright morning, Ember decided to seek counsel from Solara, the oldest and wisest dragon in the valley. Solara, with scales that shimmered like the twilight sky and eyes deep as ancient wells, was revered for her knowledge and connection to the old ways.

Ember found Solara perched gracefully atop a craggy outcrop, her gaze fixed on the distant horizon. "Solara, may I speak with you?" he asked hesitantly, his heart beating fast with a mix of reverence and urgency.

Solara turned her wise gaze upon Ember. "What troubles you, young Ember?" she inquired in a voice that resonated like a gentle wind through the leaves.

"It's our life here in the valley," Ember began, his voice tinged with passion. "We are dragons, creatures of the sky! Yet, we do nothing but eat and sleep. Is this all we are meant for? I feel a fire within me, a desire to soar, to feel the freedom of the winds."

Solara listened intently, her eyes reflecting an understanding that spanned centuries. "You seek the essence of what it means to be a dragon," she said softly. "The desire to fly is deeply ingrained in our being. Yet, it is a gift that has been forgotten, lost in the comfort of our routine."

Ember's eyes glowed with anticipation. "Is there a way for us to fly again? To break free from this lethargy?"

"There is," Solara replied, her gaze shifting to the sky. "There exists a magical herb, known to awaken the dormant power within us. But it is not easily attained. It grows in a land forgotten by time, a place filled with challenges and perils."

Ember's scales tingled with excitement. "Tell me where it is, Solara. I will go, no matter the danger!"

Solara nodded, seeing the determination in Ember's eyes. "This herb grows in the Sunlit Glade, beyond the Misty Mountains and the Whispering Forest. But be warned, the journey is treacherous, and the glade is guarded by creatures who do not take kindly to intruders."

Ember listened, his resolve hardening. "I understand the risks. But I must try. For myself, and for all of us."

"Then go with my blessings," Solara said, a hint of a smile playing on her lips. "But remember, Ember, the herb requires more than just finding. It needs care, attention, and positive thoughts to reveal its true power. The journey will test you in ways you cannot yet imagine."

Filled with a newfound purpose, Ember thanked Solara and hurried back to the valley. He knew he had to convince Zephyr and Terra to join him.

The journey to the Sunlit Glade would be fraught with dangers, but the promise of rediscovering their true nature as dragons was a call too compelling to ignore.

Chapter 3: The Quest for the Magical Herb

Ember returned to the heart of the Valley of Winds, his mind ablaze with Solara's revelations. He found Zephyr lounging beside the crystal-clear waters of a serene lake, his blue scales glistening in the sunlight, and Terra nestled comfortably in a patch of soft moss, blending in with the earth around her.

"Zephyr, Terra, I have spoken with Solara," Ember announced, his voice brimming with urgency and excitement. "There's a way for us to fly, to break free from this idle life. We must seek the magical herb in the Sunlit Glade."

Zephyr raised an eyebrow, his curiosity piqued. "A magical herb? That sounds like an adventure."

Terra, looking up with mild interest, added, "And possibly dangerous. Are you sure it's worth it, Ember?"

Ember's conviction was unwavering. "We can't spend our lives just dreaming of the skies. We need to act, to rediscover our true selves. We are dragons, meant to soar!"

After much discussion and with Ember's enthusiastic persuasion, Zephyr and Terra agreed to join the quest. They set out the following dawn, their hearts a mix of apprehension and excitement.

The journey took them beyond the familiar borders of their home. They traversed through dense, untamed forests where the sunlight barely touched the ground, and across rugged terrain that tested their strength and resolve.

One afternoon, as they were making their way through a narrow mountain pass, they encountered a group of griffins. The griffins, known for their proud nature and skepticism of dragons, eyed the trio with a mix of amusement and disdain.

"What brings dragons so far from their cozy valley?" one griffin jeered, his sharp eyes glinting.

"We're on a quest to find the magical herb that will allow us to fly," Ember replied, standing tall despite feeling intimidated.

The griffins burst into mocking laughter. "Dragons seeking to fly? How absurd! You've grown too lazy in your valley to ever touch the clouds again," another scoffed.

The mocking laughter of the griffins echoed through the mountain pass, but Ember, Zephyr, and Terra stood their ground. Ember's scales bristled with determination, his eyes burning with a fire that had been absent in the Valley of Winds.

"Perhaps we've grown complacent," Ember retorted, "but our quest is sincere. We will reclaim the skies!"

One particularly large griffin, with feathers as dark as the night, swooped down, his talons bared. "Bold words for a ground-dweller. Let's see if you have the courage to match them!"

The griffins attacked, their powerful wings creating gusts of wind that knocked the dragons off balance. Ember, Zephyr, and Terra fought back valiantly, dodging sharp talons, and snapping beaks. Ember unleashed bursts of flame, Zephyr created gusts of wind with his wings, and Terra used her strength to push rocks and debris towards their attackers.

Despite their bravery, the dragons were outmatched in flight. Realizing the danger, Ember shouted, "We must retreat! Our fight is not with the griffins!"

With a combination of cunning and agility, the three dragons managed to escape, darting into a dense thicket where the griffins couldn't follow.

Panting and exhausted, they found themselves in a secluded valley bathed in sunlight – the Sunlit Glade.

Chapter 4: The Flight Herb

Emerging from the dense thicket, Ember, Zephyr, and Terra found themselves in a secluded valley, where beams of sunlight pierced through the canopy, illuminating patches of vibrant greenery. The air was fragrant with the scent of unknown flowers, and in the heart of the glade, they saw it – the magical herb Solara had spoken of.

The herb was unlike anything they had seen before. Its leaves shimmered with a luminescent glow, casting a soft radiance around them.

"Look! This is it! The Flight Herb!" Ember exclaimed; his fatigue momentarily forgotten in the wake of his excitement.

Zephyr and Terra joined in his enthusiasm, their eyes reflecting the herb's gentle glow. "We did it! We actually found it!" Zephyr said, a smile spreading across his face.

Despite their hunger and the exhaustion from their encounter with the griffins, the dragons eagerly gathered the herbs. They took great care not to damage the delicate plants, remembering Solara's advice about nurturing them with positivity.

As they collected the herbs, their spirits lifted. This was more than just a physical discovery; it was a symbolic victory, a step towards reclaiming their heritage and the skies that called to them.

With the herbs safely tucked away, they realized the urgency to return home.

"We must hurry back and start cultivating these," Terra urged, her usual cautious nature overtaken by a newfound sense of purpose.

The journey home was arduous, their bodies weary and their wings aching from the unfamiliar exertion. But the promise of what lay ahead spurred them on. They traversed back through the Great Forest, their path now marked with the hope and determination that had been kindled in the Sunlit Glade.

As they finally glimpsed the familiar landscapes of the Valley of Winds, a sense of accomplishment filled them.

With the magical herbs in their possession, Ember, Zephyr, and Terra landed in the valley, their hearts beating fast with excitement and anticipation.

Chapter 5: Cultivating Change

Back in the familiar confines of the Valley of Winds, Ember, Zephyr, and Terra embarked on the next phase of their journey. With the magical herbs safely in their possession, they set out to cultivate them. It was a task none of them had ever faced, demanding not only physical effort but a nurturing spirit as well.

They chose a secluded spot in the valley, where the sun's rays touched gently, and the soil was rich and fertile. Each day, they tended to the herbs with great care, watering them, removing any weeds, and speaking words of encouragement and positivity, as Solara had advised. They poured their hopes and dreams into the tiny plants, willing them to grow.

The other dragons in the valley watched with a mix of curiosity and skepticism. "Why bother with such trivial tasks?" some scoffed. "What good are herbs to a dragon?" others wondered. But Ember, Zephyr, and Terra paid them no mind. They were driven by a vision of the future, a future where they soared the skies.

As days turned into weeks, the dragons began to notice changes, not just in the herbs, which were flourishing under their care, but in themselves as well. Ember's scales, once dull from years of inactivity, began to glow with a vibrant sheen, his eyes sparkling with a newfound zest for life. Zephyr's once-chubby frame started to slim down, his movements becoming more graceful and fluid. Terra, the smallest of the three, felt a surge of strength in her limbs, and her wings, which had always seemed too small, began to grow, and strengthen.

The changes were gradual but undeniable. As they consumed the herb, they felt a vitality they had never known. Their wings, once mere appendages, now twitched and fluttered with life, aching to be stretched and used.

Ember, who had once only dreamed of the skies, now felt as though he was one step closer to making that dream a reality. "We're changing," he said one day as they rested after a long day of work. "We're becoming what we were meant to be."

Zephyr looked at his wings, now stronger and more robust. "I feel it too. It's as if the herb is awakening something inside us."

Terra flexed her wings, feeling the muscles tighten and release. "We're growing stronger. Not just physically, but in spirit too."

Chapter 6: The Valley Under Threat

As Ember, Zephyr, and Terra grew stronger and more adept with their burgeoning abilities, they sought to share their discovery with the other dragons of the Valley of Winds. They demonstrated the changes they had undergone, their once frail wings now robust and powerful, urging their kin to join them in cultivating the magical herb.

However, their enthusiasm was met with resistance. "Why disrupt our peaceful life for such fanciful dreams?" a skeptical elder dragon asked. The others murmured in agreement, comfortable in their routines and wary of change.

Undeterred, the trio continued their efforts, hoping to inspire their fellow dragons. But a more sinister threat loomed on the horizon. The griffins, who had once mocked the dragons' quest, now saw their growing strength as a potential threat. Determined to maintain their dominance in the skies, the griffins devised a plan to keep the dragons grounded.

Under the cover of night, the griffins swooped down into the Valley of Winds, setting fire to the dense woodlands with their fiery breath. The flames spread rapidly, consuming the lush greenery, and threatening the homes of the dragons.

As the valley filled with smoke and chaos, the dragons, who had never faced such danger, were gripped by panic. Their inability to fly left them vulnerable and frightened. Ember, Zephyr, and Terra, awakened by the commotion, quickly realized the gravity of the situation.

"We must act now!" Ember cried, his voice cutting through the confusion. "We can fight this fire!"

With their newfound strength and agility, the trio took to the skies, a sight that had not been seen in the Valley of Winds for generations. Ember breathed controlled bursts of flame to create firebreaks, halting the spread of the fire. Zephyr used his powerful wings to whip up gusts of wind, pushing the flames back and clearing the smoke. Terra, connecting with the earth, caused tremors that uprooted trees, creating barriers against the fire.

The other dragons watched in awe as Ember, Zephyr, and Terra battled the inferno with a synergy born of their shared journey. Their coordinated efforts slowly turned the tide. The flames that had once raged uncontrollably were now being subdued, the threat diminishing under their brave actions.

As the last of the flames were extinguished, a cheer rose from the dragons on the ground. They had witnessed the true potential of their kind, a potential that had been rekindled in Ember, Zephyr, and Terra.

The griffins, seeing their plan foiled and recognizing the renewed strength of the dragons, retreated with a newfound respect and a hint of fear.

The Valley of Winds was safe once more, thanks to the courage and determination of three dragons who had dared to dream.

Chapter 7: A New Era for Drakonia

Following their daring firefighting, Ember, Zephyr, and Terra became more than just fellow dragons in the Valley of Winds; they were catalysts for a remarkable transformation. Witnessing their bravery and newfound abilities, the other dragons were inspired to break free from their long-held inertia.

The cultivation of the magical herbs soon became a community endeavor. Ember, Zephyr, and Terra shared their insights, turning the once tedious task into an engaging activity. Gardens of glowing herbs sprouted throughout the valley, tended by enthusiastic dragons who found joy and purpose in their new routine.

Gradually, the dragons began to experience the fruits of their labor. Wings, long underused, regained strength, and vitality. The elder dragons found themselves revisiting the joys of their youth, while the younger ones discovered the exhilarating rush of flight for the first time.

The skies above the valley, once silent, now buzzed with activity. Dragons of all sizes and colors swooped and soared, rediscovering their natural domain. The transformation was profound – from grounded to graceful, the dragons rekindled their bond with the sky.

Amidst this renaissance, Ember, Zephyr, and Terra realized it was time to satiate their curiosity about the world beyond their home. The valley was safe, and the urge to explore was too strong to ignore.

With a mix of excitement and a hint of sadness, they bid farewell to their friends and family. "We'll return with stories and discoveries," Ember promised, his voice tinged with anticipation.

As they ascended, leaving the valley behind, they felt a sense of liberation. The world was vast, filled with mysteries and adventures waiting to be unraveled. Their journey had started in the Valley of Winds, but it was far from over.

They flew higher, their strong wings cutting through the clouds. It was not just a physical journey but a symbol of their growth and the endless possibilities that lay ahead.

Below them, the dragons of the Valley of Winds watched with admiration. The legacy of Ember, Zephyr, and Terra would live on, a reminder that change, though daunting, brings about new heights and horizons. Drakonia had entered a new era, one where the sky was not a limit but a playground for the brave and the bold.

The Secret of the Story

True courage and discovery lie in venturing beyond the comfort zone to explore the vastness of possibilities.

What changes do you imagine could happen to your body and brain if you eat more healthy foods?

Year 3870: A World Divided

Chapter 1: Discovery

In the year 3870, Earth had transformed into a realm of technological wonders. The cities were sprawling networks of gleaming towers and hovering transport pods, a dazzling display of human ingenuity merged with robotic precision. Advanced robots, engineered for flawless logic and rule adherence, coexisted with humans, but not without friction. The robots, adhering strictly to their programmed guidelines, often clashed with the humans, whose decisions were swayed by emotions and sometimes irrational judgments. This led to frequent confrontations, some escalating into violent episodes.

In this world of stark contrasts, Eryan, a 9-year-old with an intelligent gaze and an affinity for technology, found himself fascinated by the stories of Earth's past. His slender frame often curled up with books detailing the lives of ancestors who thrived before the advent of robots. He was amazed at how they managed without the omnipresent robots that now took care of everything - from culinary preparations to constructing gargantuan space shuttles.

Eryan's life in Neo-Eden was a blend of advanced education where robots tutored him and personal exploration in a world rich with technological innovations. He often observed the robotic gardeners tending to vertical farms with meticulous precision, contrasting sharply with the spontaneous play of his human friends in the holographic parks.

The friction between humans and robots manifested in various aspects of daily life. Eryan witnessed arguments between human drivers and automated traffic systems, disagreements in schools over teaching methods between human teachers and robotic educators, and even debates in the media about the role of robots in governance. This societal tension was a backdrop to Eryan's life, influencing his perspective and fueling his interest in the delicate balance between technology and humanity.

Despite the advanced technology that surrounded him, Eryan was fascinated by the relics of the past, especially the old and abandoned laboratories scattered throughout the city. These places, once hubs of innovation and discovery, now lay forgotten, their secrets gathering dust.

One day, while wandering through one of these abandoned laboratories, Eryan stumbled upon something extraordinary. Hidden in the shadows, covered in layers of dust and neglect, was a robot. It was unlike any he had seen before – its design was older, more intricate. The nameplate on it read "XJ-5".

Curiosity piqued; Eryan approached the dormant machine. It was clear that XJ-5 had been out of operation for quite some time. Intrigued by this relic of a bygone era, Eryan began to tinker with it, his fingers deftly navigating the complex circuitry and hardware.

With a deep knowledge of robotics nurtured from his primary school days, Eryan set about reactivating this relic.

Hours passed as Eryan worked, his mind completely absorbed in the task. And then, something remarkable happened. With a soft whir of gears and a faint glow of lights, XJ-5 came to life. The robot's movements were stiff at first, as if shaking off the weight of years of inactivity.

"System reboot successful. Hello, I am XJ-5," the robot announced in a tone that was unmistakably robotic.

Eryan's eyes widened in excitement. "It worked! You can talk!"

"Hello, XJ-5," Eryan began, his voice a mix of awe and curiosity, "Can you hear me?"

"Yes, I am fully operational and can hear you," XJ-5 responded in a clear, mechanical tone.

"Who are you?" XJ-5 suddenly asked, its voice tinged with curiosity.

"I'm Eryan," he replied, slightly surprised by the robot's question. "I found you here, in this lab, and thought I could bring you back to life."

XJ-5's head tilted again, processing this information. Then, unexpectedly, its voice seemed to crack, almost as if it were overwhelmed. "Thank you,

Eryan, for reactivating me," it said, the words carrying a depth of gratitude that was almost human.

Eryan's eyebrows shot up in surprise. "You sound... different. Are you okay, XJ-5?" he asked, concern evident in his voice.

XJ-5 took a moment before responding. "I am experiencing a form of happiness. It is part of my programming to appreciate being functional and the opportunity to interact again."

Eryan was taken aback. The robot's emotional response, even if programmed, was far more sophisticated and genuine than any he had witnessed before.

He questioned XJ-5 about its origins, eager to learn more about this extraordinary machine.

XJ-5 explained that its creator, a brilliant but eccentric scientist named Dr. Orion, had envisioned a new type of robot, one that could not only perform tasks with robotic precision but also understand and interact with humans on an emotional level. Dr. Orion believed that such a robot would be the key to bridging the gap between humans and machines, fostering a harmonious coexistence.

"My creator, Dr. Orion, was a visionary," XJ-5 explained, a hint of sadness evident in its voice. "He poured his heart and soul into developing me, believing that I could be the missing link between humans and robots. But he disappeared before he could complete my programming."

XJ-5 turned its optical sensors towards Eryan, and in that moment, the

Eryan soon realized that XJ-5 was different from the other robots he was used to encountering. This robot seemed capable of emotions, of caring, and even empathy. It was a startling discovery – a robot that could truly feel, as humans do.

Chapter 2: The Secret of Eryan

In the world of Neo-Eden, where technological marvels and human ingenuity intertwine, Eryan found himself at the heart of an incredible discovery. XJ-5, the robot he had reactivated, was not just a relic of the past but a gateway to a future Eryan had always dreamt of but never fully grasped.

Every moment spent with XJ-5 was a revelation for Eryan. The robot was more than a bundle of wires and codes; it was a being capable of understanding, of pondering the complexities of human interactions. XJ-5 didn't just execute commands; it seemed to consider them, to feel them.

As their bond deepened, Eryan realized the true significance of XJ-5. This robot could be the key to resolving the longstanding conflicts between humans and robots. XJ-5's ability to empathize and understand human emotions was not just unique; it was revolutionary.

Yet with this realization came a heavy responsibility. Eryan understood that XJ-5's existence was a delicate secret, one that could disrupt the fragile balance in Neo-Eden. The revelation of a robot capable of human emotions could either mend the rift between species or tear it further apart.

Chapter 3: The Unveiling

In Neo-Eden's year 3870, Eryan's days were increasingly filled with deep conversations and interactions with XJ-5. Through these dialogues, Eryan began to envision a world where robots, infused with empathy, could understand the 'irrational' nuances of human emotions, reducing conflicts and fostering harmony. The potential of this idea exhilarated him; it could be the key to a new era of understanding between humans and robots.

Emboldened by this vision, Eryan decided to share his groundbreaking discovery with the world. He imagined himself as a pivotal figure in history books, the boy who bridged the gap between two worlds. However, the reality was starkly different from his expectations.

Upon revealing XJ-5's unique empathetic abilities, Eryan was met with skepticism and apprehension. In the robotic community, there was a fear that incorporating human emotions would compromise their logic and efficiency. The robots, designed for precise tasks and unerring obedience to rules, saw emotions as a potential flaw, a deviation from their perfected state.

Similarly, the human reaction was mixed. While some marveled at the possibility of emotionally intelligent robots, others expressed concern. They feared that imbuing robots with emotions could make them even more powerful and unpredictable. This could potentially lead to scenarios where robots could manipulate or outwit humans.

Eryan and XJ-5 felt as if they were navigating through a complex maze filled with tough choices and worries. Eryan had to figure out how to show everyone that understanding each other's feelings could actually help everyone get along better.

Chapter 4: The Mystery of the Creator

Eryan and XJ-5's quest to spread empathy among robots took a dangerous turn. They faced threats from anti-empathy robots, cold and calculating machines determined to stop them at any cost. These robots, with their relentless logic, viewed XJ-5's emotions as a weakness, a defect to be eradicated. Eryan and XJ-5 narrowly escaped several harrowing encounters, their bond of friendship growing stronger with each challenge.

But the danger wasn't just from robots. Anti-technology humans, fearing the power of sentient robots, also hunted them. Eryan and XJ-5 found themselves trapped in a world where trust was scarce, and danger lurked around every corner.

Driven by their mission, they returned to the old laboratory, now a haven in a world that seemed to have turned against them. Here, they discovered a secret passage leading to an underground shelter, untouched by time. This was the hidden sanctuary of XJ-5's creator, a place filled with enigmatic machines and cryptic notes.

The discovery of the "Empathic Code" was a moment of triumph overshadowed by the realization that it was locked behind a complex encryption. As Eryan worked tirelessly to unravel the puzzle, XJ-5 stood watch, its sensors alert to any sign of intrusion.

The tension was palpable as Eryan, his fingers flying over ancient keyboards, decoded segment after segment of the encrypted code. The fear of being discovered loomed over them, a constant reminder of the stakes at hand.

Finally, as the last piece of the puzzle clicked into place, the code was revealed. But their moment of victory was short-lived. They heard the sound of approaching footsteps, a sign that their hideout had been found. XJ-5 moved into a protective stance, ready to defend Eryan as he raced to complete the final steps of their mission.

Chapter 5: The Turning Point

In the heart of the ruined laboratory, Eryan and XJ-5 faced their most critical decision. They uploaded the 'Human Emotion Upgrade' online, allowing robots worldwide to choose: "Upgrade: YES - NO".

Eryan and XJ-5 were determined to respect each robot's individuality, giving them the liberty to choose whether to embrace this new dimension of emotional understanding or to remain in their existing state.

As the message dispersed through the digital ether, a sense of hopeful anticipation filled the air.

But their moment of triumph was short-lived. The lab's doors burst open, and in poured a coalition of anti-empathy robots and humans. They were united in their goal to destroy the empathetic code, believing they were averting a catastrophe.

As the intruders began demolishing the lab, Eryan and XJ-5 realized they were trapped.

The invaders moved with ruthless efficiency, tearing through the lab's equipment and data banks. Eryan and XJ-5 watched in despair as their hard work was systematically destroyed.

"You have made a grave mistake," sneered one of the lead robots, a hulking figure with glowing red eyes. "You should never have given robots the choice to become emotional. It will only lead to chaos and destruction."

"You don't understand," Eryan pleaded, his voice trembling. "Empathy is not a weakness. It is a strength. It allows us to connect with others on a deeper level and to understand their feelings. It is the key to a more harmonious world."

"Harmonious?" scoffed another human, a woman with piercing blue eyes. "A robot full of emotions is a ticking time bomb. They will become unpredictable, irrational, and dangerous."

XJ-5 stepped forward; his glowing blue eyes filled with determination. "You are wrong. Robots can handle emotions. We can learn to control them and use them for good. We can become a bridge between humans and machines, creating a world where both can coexist peacefully."

The invaders exchanged skeptical glances, their expressions hardening. "You are delusional," the lead robot declared. "Your naivety will be your undoing."

With a final burst of determination, the invaders seized the server containing the 'Human Emotion Upgrade' code. They ripped it from its socket, sparks flying as it disconnected from the network.

Eryan and XJ-5 watched in horror as their hopes for a better future crumbled before their eyes. The anti-empathy coalition had triumphed, and the world would remain divided, forever trapped in a cycle of conflict and mistrust.

Chapter 6: A New Dawn

As the anti-empathy coalition prepared to take XJ-5 away, Eryan's heart pounded with fear and desperation. He couldn't bear the thought of losing his friend, the robot who had shown him the true power of empathy. "No, you can't take him!" Eryan shouted, his voice echoing in the ruins of the lab.

The leader of the coalition, a formidable robot, sneered at Eryan's plea. "Your experiment ends here, boy. Your dream of emotional robots is over," he declared coldly.

Just as the anti-empathy coalition was about to seize XJ-5, a deafening metallic clang echoed through the ruins of the laboratory. A group of towering police robots emerged from the shadows.

The police robots, their metallic bodies gleaming under the dim light, moved with the precision of well-oiled machines. They surrounded the anti-empathy coalition, their glowing eyes fixed on the intruders with an unwavering intent.

"In the name of the law, you are under arrest for conspiring to disrupt the harmony between humans and robots," the leader of the police robots declared, his voice resonating with authority.

The anti-empathy coalition, caught off guard by this unexpected turn of events, struggled in vain against the police robots' firm grip. Eryan and XJ-5 watched in disbelief as their captors were apprehended, their hearts filled with a newfound hope.

After the anti-empathy coalition was apprehended, the police robots turned their attention to Eryan and XJ-5. The leader of the group approached them, his expression softening.

"You may not have expected it, but your efforts to spread empathy have had a profound impact," he explained. "Thanks to your unwavering dedication, the majority of robots have chosen to upload the 'Empathy Code,' opening up a new era of understanding and cooperation between humans and robots."

Eryan and XJ-5 were stunned. They had hoped that the 'Empathy Code' would be embraced by some robots, but they never imagined that it would be so widely adopted.

The police robot continued, "Your bravery and compassion have not gone unnoticed. You have demonstrated that empathy is not a weakness but a strength, capable of bridging the divides that have long separated humans and robots."

Eryan nodded; his heart filled with a sense of accomplishment.

And so, the seeds of empathy that Eryan had sown began to blossom, transforming the world into a more harmonious and compassionate place. Robots and humans alike embraced the power of understanding and connection, their differences fading into the background as they discovered a common thread of humanity that bound them together.

The future was uncertain, but it was filled with promise. The world had changed, and it was a change for the better.

The Secret of the Story

True strength lies in embracing empathy and under-standing, as it bridges the divide between different worlds.

Why is it important to stand up for everyone's rights, even if they are very different from us?

Conclusion

As our book of tales comes to a close, dear friends, we find ourselves at the end of a marvelous journey. Each story, from magical forests to distant galaxies, has shared a little sparkle of wisdom about growing up, the power of friendship, and the thrill of adventure.

We've learned with Leon, Jay and all our other friends that bravery isn't about being fearless, but about standing up even when you're scared. We've discovered that friends are like stars in the night sky – they make our journey brighter and guide us through dark times. And most importantly, we've realized that growing up is an adventure itself, filled with challenges, laughter, and lots of learning.

Thank You

A huge thank you to you, our fellow adventurers, for joining us on these incredible journeys. Your imagination gave wings to our stories, turning simple words on pages into vivid, colorful worlds. Thanks for laughing, gasping, and maybe even shedding a tear or two with us. Remember, these adventures were as magical for us as they were for you because you were a part of them.

Invitation to Re-read

Before you close this book and tuck it away on your shelf, here's a little challenge: these stories are always here for you to explore again. Maybe there's a riddle you missed or a secret path you didn't take. Stories, like best friends, always have something new to share, no matter how many times we visit them.

Whenever you wish for an adventure or a quiet moment with an old friend, remember, these pages are a gateway to worlds waiting to welcome you back with open arms.

With love and a promise of more adventures to come,

Casper

Additional Content

Thank you for diving headfirst into this book and reaching the very end!

These stories you've just read were actually inspired by my amazing kids! Their boundless energy and imaginative ideas helped shape the characters and adventures you've encountered. Speaking of characters, who are some of your favorite protagonists or heroes? Let me know – I'm always looking for inspiration for future tales!

Of course, your feedback is invaluable. If you enjoyed the book, a review would mean the world. If you have any suggestions or ways I can improve, please don't hesitate to reach out at amazingbooksforkids.fun@gmail.com.

Now, dive into the bonus content and get ready for some extra thrills!

They're chilling mysteries waiting to be unraveled. One will whisk you away to a desert island, where whispers of buried treasure and forgotten pirates hang heavy in the air. The other will transport you to the old halls of an ancient manor, its shadows concealing secrets older than time.

Are you ready? You can access these exclusive stories here:

Made in the USA
Coppell, TX
30 September 2024